DRAGON'S SACRIFICE

Chloe Knight

CHAPTER 1 - DATE NIGHT

"Are you sure this really is a good idea?" I whined. I leaned back into a dramatic slouch and turned my best pleading look to my husband in the driver's seat. We were speeding through the city, weaving around the few vehicles that were braving the road. It was considered bad luck to travel during a monsoon, a superstition held over from history when the protective barrier over the city was prone to failing and there was a risk of water pouring into the city with lethal force.

Rowan took his focus off the road long enough to give me an impatient glare. The glare was accented by a scowl that made the scar on his lip more predominant, and the scar near his eye pucker slightly, making him look more threatening than he actually was. It didn't remotely intimidate me. I knew him far too well.

I quickly resumed my pleading look and added a pouty lip for good measure.

"Hope, my love, my angel, my darling," he said with the strained tone that informed me that my theatrical whining had continued too long, and I was truly getting on his nerves.

I gave him a cheeky, lip biting grin. Actually, annoying Rowan was difficult. He was the most patient, compassionate man I knew, and I was a little proud that I had succeeded.

He sighed loudly and turned his attention back to the road. "You know, it isn't like this is the first time you've left them."

True, he wasn't wrong. I was the Honored Companion to the Crown Princess of Valoria, a position too important and high profile to offer infinite maternity leave. I had actually returned to all of my duties a few weeks ago. I couldn't even claim my unease was due to any kind of premonition, my telepathy had a far more sinister focus, and I lacked the ability to learn the Oracle craft. Still, when we left the twins with their nannies, I felt something was horrifyingly wrong, and I had the overwhelming desire to take them out of the nursery and run away. I still couldn't shake the feeling that fleeing was the only way to keep my girls safe.

The paranoia was so absurd that Rowan was convinced a night out would be good for me. Our daughters were safe in the secure high rise that also housed the royal family and other high-ranking nobles like my husband. There was nowhere on Karabeeya safer, and my paranoia was probably proof I needed a real break. Truthfully, I agreed with Rowan's assessment, but it wasn't going to stop me from complaining the entire way to the restaurant.

Curious as to how far I could push Rowan now that he was already visibly annoyed, I switched tactics. "Well, are we there yet?" I asked brightly.

Rowan's only response was to huff impatiently and shake his head, although he couldn't quite conceal the smile that threatened to break across his face.

Realizing he had caught on to my antics, I relaxed against the seat and laughed. Rowan and I were soulmates, the rare pairing of two people who were perfectly compatible and bound with an unbreakable bond. When that compatibility grew into love, and the basis for our marriage, I realized that it meant Rowan needed my immaturity and irritating quirks. They kept him from taking himself too seriously.

I relaxed marginally as Rowan slowed down and pulled into a small parking lot. We weren't far from the girls. If there was an emergency, we could get back to them in less than fifteen minutes.

"Alright, we're here," Rowan sighed as he parked in front of a perfectly round building made of iridescent glass. I frowned at the building, half expecting it to roll down the slight incline and smash into our car.

Even though I hadn't felt any vibrations warning me of an incoming message, I still took my screen out of my bag and checked it. No messages lit up at all, not that I would expect to see one from the nannies. I reminded myself that both nannies were competent, and trustworthy. I needed to calm down so I could relax and enjoy this rare chance to spend time alone with Rowan. Not Rowan and the kids, or Rowan and the Royals, but just Rowan.

I looked around as Rowan climbed out of the car and walked around it to my door. There were no other vehicles in the parking lot, no pedestrians on the walkways or lingering near the buildings. The superstition about the barrier was more prevalent this evening than usual.

My door swung up, poised on the vehicle like a butterfly wing. Rowan stood next to the car and held out his hand. I bit my lip and grinned. He was so easy to tease, and so unrelentingly chivalrous. I took his hand and climbed out of the car.

Normally, I stepped out of the car and moved to his side in a single graceful motion. This time I hesitated outside the car as I was overwhelmed again by the desire to climb back into the car and return home so Rowan and I could take my children and flee. That hesitation put me too close to the door when it closed. The door caught one of the charms on my bracelet. My hand was yanked down as the door crushed the charm and trapped me against the vehicle.

Seeing the problem immediately, Rowan opened the door. I stepped away from it, so he could safely close it, and surveyed the damage on the charm. The bracelet was a gift from my adopted mother, an oracle named Millenia. I had learned that the charms on it were not mere decoration. The tiny key opened Millenia's journal, a book of prophesies, and the folded blade concealed within the band of the bracelet had helped with countless inconveniences. I couldn't guess the usefulness of the other charms, but I didn't doubt they were each more than decoration. Millennia was too thorough for that.

The charm that had caught in the door frame was a perfect crystal sphere encased in a cage made of elaborately twisted silver wire. The cage was bent practically in half, splitting the once smooth, flawless crystal into two pieces, each caught in part of the cage.

I chewed on my lip as I surveyed the damage and realized the cage's design couldn't be fixed or duplicated without a reference.

Did I have an image of that charm? Perhaps a fortunate angle in a photo or video? The cage had been truly beautiful.

"I'll order you another crystal," Rowan said, misunderstanding the source of my annoyance. "Were you hurt?"

I shook my head and twisted the cage to look at the other side. "I'm fine. I don't need another crystal, I'll just ask a jeweler to fix the cage, if I can find an image for reference. He can just repair the crystal. The break looks clean, a little glue and it will be hardly noticeable."

Rowan stiffened, his jaw jutted out slightly, as he did when we were about to argue. I waited as he mentally shifted through the arguments until he finally settled on what exactly he wanted to say. It was a process I was familiar with, both as a witness and a participant in the arguments.

"You shouldn't carry a damaged colalace crystal, it defeats the purpose."

I examined the pieces of the crystal with new interest. So, it wasn't the design of the cage that was important, it was the crystal inside the cage.

"What is a colalace crystal and what does it do?" I asked. I poked at the crystal half and noticed a slight prismatic shine on the damaged portion.

"It's also called a healer's crystal. It can heal any injury, if the victim is still alive. It's an excruciating process, they say the one being healed feels the pain of the injury all over again. To some accounts the pain is tenfold. Some planets have passed laws limiting the use of these crystals. To use one without adequate painkillers is considered illegal torture, unless in the most extreme circumstances."

I shook my head and stopped toying with the broken cage protecting the crystal pieces. "I am a healer. If someone is hurt, I would use my magic to heal them. I don't need a crystal." I didn't add that I could heal someone without them being forced to endure the torment of their injury all over again as I healed them.

"Unless your magic is drained," Rowan pointed out with a smirk.

I returned his smirk with one of my own. He was right, and if Millenia felt the need to give me one of these crystals, there was a strong chance I would someday need it.

"So now that it's broken, it's completely useless?" I asked as we walked toward the sphere-shaped building.

Rowan reluctantly shook his head. "The crystal will still heal, but any flaw in the crystal will cause a backlash that will result in blindness."

I stopped and Rowan turned to look at me curiously. "Blindness?" I asked. "What a random penalty for the magic in the crystal. I've heard of artifact backlash that matches the power amplified, like a heat stone burning the user or a communication pool creating feedback that can cause hearing loss or even brain damage, but I haven't heard of a magical artifact causing an unrelated injury."

"It's not as random a penalty as it sounds. The backlash of the magic primarily damages the part of the brain that interprets sight. Essentially, the user loses the ability to interpret the signals the eyes send to the brain. It's completely irreversible, and even implants can't correct the damage."

I studied the crystal with new reluctance. "Well then, I guess I better replace this crystal, so I'm never tempted to use it." Although, I wouldn't get rid of this damaged one until I had the replacement. I would gladly trade eyesight to save Rowan, or any of our daughters in the event of a life-threatening injury.

"The crystals exist only on Talaraine. I will place an order, but it will take two or three days for the replacement to arrive," Rowan promised. He took my hand, tangling his fingers in mine. Talaraine was the other habitable planet in our solar system.

Talaraine was also the home of my parents, people I had never met and who didn't know I was alive thanks to my evil grandmother faking my death when I was an infant.

"It's not like I need it immediately," I joked, eager to shift the conversation away from Talaraine. "After all, I'm just being paranoid tonight."

"You're being something," Rowan grumbled as he led me to the door.

The round door spun to the side, creating a prism as the streetlights reflected off the faceted edges of the moving door.

As I watched the door, I leaned against Rowan. "This place is extremely ostentatious, why did you choose it?"

"Crowe recommended it, I've never been here, but apparently it's popular," Rowan said.

"I can't picture Crowe coming here either," I stated as we stepped into the building. Crowe was one of Prince Remy's personal guards, and a good friend, who hated being the center of attention. He was the type who went to relaxing, quiet places, not glitzy obnoxious places like this restaurant.

I looked around, the sphere theme continued inside, giving the impression of tiny bubbles within a large bubble that distorted the city lights. It was also completely empty.

"Rowan, if this restaurant is so popular, where is everyone?" I asked. I released his hand. "You didn't rent the entire place out for some surprise?"

Rowan looked around. "No," he whispered. "That wouldn't have been a bad idea, but I didn't think of it."

I nodded and thinned my mental wall, the barrier that kept my telepathy in check and normally prevented me from reading the minds and emotions of others. As soon as the wall thinned, I felt an attempted invasion, a force attempting to read my mind as I had tried to search for others in the building. In that instant, I strengthened my wall, cutting off the other telepath, but also making it impossible to search for other minds.

CHAPTER 2 –
SACRIFICE

"Rowan don't lower your defenses, there is another telepath here," I hissed. I took a knife out of my purse and held it in one hand and kept my purse in the other. It was heavy enough to throw at someone if a momentary distraction was needed. Rowan's telepathic control was better than mine, so I did not need to worry about him turning against me as the other telepath's marionette.

I stepped forward. The room was perfectly round, but smaller than the outside of the building, and there was no sign of a kitchen. The telepath had to be in the kitchen, but there wasn't another door that I could see, everything was seamless.

I wasted precious time searching the walls, and didn't see the seven Nexan Hunters, the elite of my grandfather's soldiers, until they dropped from the ceiling. Rowan took a small knife out of the sheath under his jacket and charged it with his magic, causing electricity to spike along the blade.

I tried not to chuckle. Why didn't I realize magic could get us out of this? I was still in the mindset of not using my magic near loved ones, although my control had grown significantly in the past year. I charged my purse with my own special kind of explosive magic and threw it at the three hunters in front of us. When it struck the middle hunter's arm, he had moved to block it, the purse exploded and pushed all three of them back.

As the Hunters' attention was drawn to the explosion, I

whipped my knife at the closest hunter, driving it towards her neck. She wasn't ready for my knife, a stupid mistake that cost her life.

Her companion screamed with pure agony and threw a blast of magic at me. I threw my knife at her, right before the magic hit me. I flew back, my torso engulfed in green fire. I landed on the ground with a sense of weakness and wrongness. I tried to move my hand, but I was too weak. Moving my legs wasn't an option, I couldn't feel anything below my chest. Perhaps it was a good thing I couldn't move my head, so I couldn't see what damage the green fire caused. My shoulders were wet, my hands and arms were drenched in sticky blood. It wasn't painful, and that was the worst part, knowing I had been on fire and should have felt *something.* I needed to focus on something other than the realization that half of me might be completely gone.

"Hope!" Rowan screamed. He appeared in my blurry vision. He looked at my face, then down at my torso with wide, tear-filled eyes and a face that was unnaturally pale. He spent too long staring at my torso.

I wanted to say his name, but even just breathing was so hard, and getting harder with each passing moment. I tried to at least whisper his name, but my face was growing numb, and my lips didn't move, no matter how much I wanted them to.

Rowan grabbed my wrist, the grip painful. His gaze focused on my face, deliberately keeping his attention away from the damage the magic blast had done to the rest of me.

He smiled through his tears, although his chin trembled, and the smile reflected fear and grief.

"I love you, Hope," he whispered, his voice cracked on my name.

I tried to smile, to let him know in some small way that I appreciated him staying with me, that I loved him as much as he loved me. I had to communicate that sentiment, because breathing was no longer possible, and my awareness was fading quickly.

Then fire erupted from my wrist and spread down to my torso. The pain was ongoing, far worse than the flash of pain caused by the green fire.

The pain grew, and I found I was able to gasp, my ability to breath restored, but before I could appreciate it, the pain intensified. I screamed and arched my back. The pain took over every nerve, every part of me was on fire, my torso was the worst, but there was no relief. Then, as I hoped for death, the pain vanished. I gasped and moved my leg but couldn't muster the energy to sit up. I squeezed Rowan's hand. I was grateful I could still feel his hand in mine.

Rowan chuckled with relief and gently squeezed my hand back. I moved my head to meet his eyes. He wasn't looking at me, his gaze was over my shoulder, at the floor.

"Rowan," I gasped. I moved my hand and realized he held the hand with the bracelet.

The damaged colalace crystal.

I was healed from what was likely a mortal injury, with my damaged colalace crystal, and Rowan wasn't looking at me because it was impossible for him to see anything.

"Are you okay?" I whispered, my voice cracking on the last word.

Once again Rowan tried to smile, although it looked more like a strained wince. "I should be asking you that question," he choked.

I heard a shuffle. I turned to my right as the Hunter who blasted me with the green fire climbed back to her feet. She took a few steps towards us, my bloody knife in her hand. I tensed, still too weak to do anything.

The Hunter stumbled, blood poured down her neck right before she fell forward, revealing the hunter behind her, and Megaera.

"I was very clear, do not harm my granddaughter," she said complacently as she walked past the body.

Megaera hadn't aged, not since the day she turned twenty, and while we were both from races that had long lives, she truly looked younger than I did, despite being older than my grandfather, her favorite lover. Her thick black hair was loose, and fell nearly to her knees, and her skin was sickeningly pale. I had heard all my life that she was beautiful, but I only saw the monster that still haunted my nightmares.

Megaera raised her hand in a lazy gesture, and Rowan rose off the floor and into the air. He reached for his neck, gasping. I tried to push off the floor, but no matter my desperation, I could not move. I simply did not have the strength.

Megaera tilted her head as she studied Rowan.

"You saved my granddaughter's life, sacrificing your eyesight in the process. You may live." With a flick of her wrist, she sent Rowan flying across the room and into the curved wall.

I gasped as I felt my body lift off the floor, every muscle frozen against my will as I was suspended above the floor like the specter in some cheap magic trick.

"Hope, my favorite grandchild," Megaera said fondly. I couldn't move, couldn't even close my eyes as she approached me. She pressed her hand affectionately against my face. I wanted to flinch, to get away from her, but even if I was strong enough to run away from her, it wouldn't have made a difference.

CHAPTER 3 -PRISON

Sleep induced by Megaera's telepathy was the worst. Not only was it not particularly restful, but it caused nightmares that I couldn't escape until Megaera allowed it. I even knew I was dreaming, but there was no escaping the cycle of entrapment, loss, and desperation.

I found myself trapped in a bathroom filled with smoke, but just when I broke out, I fell into a lake filled with blood. Kayda sat on the shore, blood trickling down the side of her head into the lake. I tried to wade through the blood toward the shore, but I never made progress, and Kayda never wavered in her unblinking, condemning glare.

I tripped and fell into the horrifying liquid, and continued to fall, and fall, sinking ever deeper into the thick blood. I choked and the temperature continued to rise.

Finally free to gasp, and open my eyes, then rapidly blinked away tears. There was no way to know how long I had been trapped in the cycle of shifting nightmares, but I woke tired, and disoriented. At least I was strong enough to climb to my feet from the cold damp floor.

The room was completely bare, except for a grate in the floor in the corner, likely for waste. My dress, or what had been left of it, had been replaced with a simple black shirt and shorts, and all my jewelry, including my hair pins, were gone, leaving only a bracelet that restricted my magic and stunted my healing ability.

I took a slow deep breath. I had been in a room like this before. I knew the entrance was a panel in the wall, carefully concealed and impossible to open from the side. My deep breath had confirmed that the air was tainted, a chemical to keep me tired and compliant. The key difference was this time, it was silent, void of the wails and tormented cries of the other prisoners.

Rather than uselessly shout or strike the walls in a futile attempt to find the exit, I slowly began to stretch. The calm motions would annoy my guards, while also keeping me occupied.

Time was difficult to track, the light never dimmed, but after I stretched to the point of complete exhaustion, and took a nap, food was pushed through a small slit that appeared in the wall and vanished as soon as the food was through.

The tray contained a shallow bowl of lukewarm mush that I guzzled quickly before the faint yeasty taste made me gag. It wasn't nearly enough to sate my hunger, but the last time I was there, I had been in the room until I was little more than a skeleton draped in cracked skin, and I knew I needed whatever nourishment my captors would provide, no matter how gross.

The water I drank less eagerly. It was a familiar shade of murky gray, and when I finally took a sip, it had a bitter aftertaste that even the chemical in the air didn't mask. After the clear, slightly sweet water I had grown accustomed to on Karabeeya, this water was nasty. The water confirmed that I wasn't on a Nexan spaceship. On the spaceships, the water was tasteless and repeatedly recycled. I grew up on Nexa, in the underground capital where the bitter, gray water was the only available water.

I finished the water, the motion giving me the chance to get my facial expressions under control. I wasn't going to cry, not in a prison where my every move was monitored by concealed cameras.

Nexa was a desert world where all inhabitants lived underground. In the extensive caverns, life could grow, but little flourished. Instead, Nexa attacked other worlds for the resources needed, and even forged some alliance that gave them the power to fight the Amaranthian Empire. My grandfather was the Prince of Nexa, a cruel dictator who ordered the execution of not only any traitor, but their families as well. Although, if memory served, my grandfather's insane lover had left my husband on Karabeeya, which didn't fit with their normal method of dealing with traitors like me.

I truly thought they were going to starve me so I was too weak to use my telepathy without the bracelet and would therefore be easier to interrogate. Fortunately, it was only four meals until there was a change.

I was asleep when the door opened, and that didn't wake me, but the footsteps did.

I opened my eyes, and sat up, but stayed on the floor, so she would have to drag me if I decided not to go with her. She bore a remarkable resemblance to Megaera. While all of Megaera's clones all shared her DNA, there were modifications to each. Some were telepaths, others wielded different magic, and none had her cunning.

It was an effective army.

"Who are you?" I whispered. Most of the clone didn't have names, but some of the more intelligent ones claimed names or were given names.

"I am a worthy Priestess of the Goddess of Life."

I rolled my eyes at the unnecessary reminder that my delusional grandmother seemed to truly believe she was a deity and used a few of her clones as enforcers of the cult she created. The general population of Nexa either believed she was the Goddess of Life, or they convincingly pretended they did so they could stay alive.

"By the command of the Goddess, you will come with me," the priestess ordered coldly.

"Nah, I'm comfortable right here," I said casually. I sat up and moved to the wall. I leaned against the wall and smiled up at the priestess. Now I would learn if this particular clone was telekinetic, and if she was strong enough to move me at my most obstinate. In preparation, I slumped, letting every muscle relax.

Disappointingly, she didn't even try to forcefully move me out of the cell. She simply huffed and walked out of the room, the panel sealing behind her.

I smirked at the wall. Megaera could be cruelly creative with her punishments, but I had been through this imprisonment before, I could handle anything she did to me.

I expected to wait for days, at the very least so I would be starved and too weak to put up a real fight, but when the door opened a few minutes later, it was clear the priestess was only going to get another clone.

It was harder to say what was different about this woman from Megaera, just tiny differences that said they weren't the same person, although the second clone looked a lot more like Megaera than the first.

"You will follow us of your own accord, or you will be subjected to telepathic persuasion," the priestess said icily.

"Who's your friend?" I asked, stalling. I wasn't stupid. With the bracelet, and my current exhaustion, I wouldn't be able to resist telepathic control from a half-trained child.

"I am a worthy priestess of the Goddess of Life," the second woman announced loftily. "I am also a skilled telepath, fully capable of overriding your defenses long enough to get you to our glorious goddess."

"Only because I'm wearing this bracelet. Take it off, see if you really are strong enough to overpower my defenses."

"The bracelet will remain in place. I will not remove the bracelet and return your power to you, no matter how you goad me. To do so would be an act of treason against my Goddess, as would allowing you to linger when she commands you to join her for a meeting."

"All right," I sighed. All I wanted was to know where I was going, and it sounded like I was going to be taken straight to Megaera. I climbed to my feet and smirked at the two women. "I'll name you Sycophant, and you Flunky," I said pointing first to the telepath, then to the first priestess. "Lead the way ladies."

Sycophant glanced at Flunky before she walked out in the hallway. Flunky walked behind me, letting me know that even with the bracelet, they treated me like I was still a real threat.

As we walked, I was able to confirm that this was the same

cold metal hallway as the prisons in the Nexan Central Government Compound. I wasn't just on Nexa, I was in the same building I grew up in.

Perfect. I had escaped this building once. I could do it again.

They led me into a small interrogation room, nothing more than two chairs on either side of a table that was bolted to the floor.

"Sit," Flunky ordered.

I wanted to argue, but I noticed a telepath pressing against the mental wall I kept up. This one was not strengthened by my telepathy, but a mere mental control Rowan taught me. If Megaera put enough effort into her own telepathy, she could overwhelm my weakened mental wall. Instead, of letting her keep beating against the mental wall, I stopped fighting and sat down. I even let the clones shackle me to the chair without resistance.

They didn't stay. Instead, they walked out of the room as Megaera walked in. She was dressed in her full regalia, an elaborate headdress made from elaborate tangles of delicate gem encrusted chains. The chains were part of her dress and tangled around her neck and arms. The dress was white, billowing silk. She sat in the chair across from mine.

I rattled the shackles and smirked at her. "Are you still afraid of me?"

"You are coming into your powers, slowly. I'll confess they were not what I was expecting."

"I was born a telepath, and I've been using the same abilities I developed when I was six. I not 'coming' into anything," I laughed. It was absurd! I was a stronger telepath than her, and I knew it. Full strength, I could easily fool Megaera. As long as I didn't slip and lose control than my power of course.

"Your powers as a Goddess," Megaera clarified archly. "I truly believed you were the Goddess of War. I would have motivated you differently if I had known the truth."

I clenched my jaw. Her claim that I was a Goddess was nothing new. It was the justification for all her torture and taking over my mind to force me to do horrifying things as her personal puppet. Unforgivable things, like mutilating my cousin Kayda in front of my sister, Phoenix.

"This feels like the same motivation, actually," I said through gritted teeth. I rattled the shackles and sat back to better glare at her.

Megaera gave a delicate, mournful sigh and shook her head, artfully moving the headdress so the gems caught the light in a hypnotic pattern.

"I had to wear down your defenses. I had to be sure when you spoke to me, it was only with the truth."

I winced, hoping it looked genuine. Megaera thought she was equal to Prince Setne in her ability to discern truth from lie, but she lacked the necessary level of empathy to be truly successful. With her particular focus of telepathy, she could implant a suggestion that would make it harder for me to want to lie to her, but fortunately, she did not admit her shortcoming to herself, and therefore could be tricked.

It would only work if I was very careful. It was going to be a very difficult con to pull off in my weakened state. I would have to start with misdirection, sometime a distraction was all it took to derail and interrogation.

"I thought you didn't like it when your clones looked too much like you, out of concern that the wrong woman would be worshipped and all that," I said.

"Their predecessors were inadequate, as were the acolytes pulled from the population of this planet. These priestesses are perfection and perform exactly to my requirements."

"I take it the predecessors and acolytes are all dead. Did you kill them for being inadequate?"

She lowered her eyes in the perfect mimicry of downcast sadness. "Culling them was an unfortunate necessity, a natural consequence of failure."

She gave a few seconds of her performance, then gracefully stood up and met my gaze with her false love.

She stood. "Please, excuse me."

She stepped to the door, which was behind me, and I couldn't turn enough to see what was going on. She returned with a screen in one carefully manicured hand.

"You, young goddess, are infuriating," Megaera said. She held up the screen so I could see the image. My oldest daughter, Athena, crying alone in her room. Megaera shifted the image to one of Rowan holding one of the twins. His eyes were bandaged.

"What do you want," I asked sullenly. My family should have been safe, and she should have never been able to get close enough to get surveillance images of them in our home.

"Give me a number between one and five," Megaera commanded.

I froze. I had seen her play this particular game before, but I had never been on the receiving end of it.

"Two," I said, knowing full well the number itself didn't matter.

There was a pause, as it dragged on, a part of me was stupid enough to hope that her plan wouldn't work, that she was bluffing and any second, she would put me back in a telepathy induced sleep while she came up with another tactic.

It was foolish, and only after I dared embrace my hopeful daydream did reality shatter around me as Megaera once again turn the screen to face me.

On the screen was Athena, stubborn, proud Athena, scowling as she held up two fingers.

"Guess another one," Megaera prompted. "This…stepdaughter… of yours will comply, I have no doubt of that." She said stepdaughter with a halting, painful tone.

"I get it, I snapped, unable to look away from my daughter. She was turning twelve soon, or possibly she already had. "Which one of the nannies works for you?"

"That information is not relevant to you. The only information you need is what it is going to take to ensure this girl's continued survival. I will confess, the twins are of great interest to me, but this child you adopted. This pretender in the Royal House of Deva who lacks the blood of my beloved in her veins? Her death will mean nothing at all."

"Her death would matter to me," I said through gritted teeth.

"I am aware. I am also aware that the Goddess of Loyalty could be a valuable asset within the Royal House of Deva. The question is, how powerful are you truly, and what are your limits?"

This again? "I'm not a goddess. There is no such thing as a living deity. That just something delusional people like you claim to convince entire planets to submit to your cruelty."

"You think I'm delusional?" Megaera asked idly. "It's *your* delusions that are exhausting, and we will need to break through, if you want this girl to live through the next two Nexan months."

"I can't give you the information you want, I don't have it! I am no more the Goddess of Loyalty than the Goddess of War." When I returned to Karabeeya I would slap Amara for spreading her theory where Megaera's spies could learn of it. According to Amara, what Megaera called Gods were actually vessels for the magic of the deities. The vessels were chosen from birth, to hold the power and to use it when there was a great need in the universe. When the vessel had fulfilled their purpose, another vessel was born, and either the previous vessel could surrender their power to the new, their power would pass to the new vessel on their death, or they could kill the new vessel and gain even more power, even as they twisted their power to selfish ends. According to Amara, that was exactly what Megaera had done for centuries.

Considering Amara claimed she was the Goddess of Love, and thought I was the Goddess of Loyalty, I figured she was just as crazy as Megaera, albeit relatively harmless.

"What do you really want?" I asked. "Two months is a strangely specific timeline."

Megaera nodded once. "I believe we can learn of your power and limitations as you help me with a family matter."

I glanced down at the image of Athena.

"We have found Princess Phoenix," Megaera said.

I *barely* managed to keep my face clear of any reaction.

My sister had managed to escape then. I knew she was smart enough to escape whatever hell our grandparents threw her in.

"And you want me for what exactly? I'm not exactly her favorite person."

"It's said, in ancient times the Goddess of Loyalty could inspire devotion in others, it's an ability you have demonstrated in the past."

Slaves, I could turn people into slaves of my will. It was Megaera's specialty and one she had developed in me.

"Phoenix is immune to telepathic control," I snapped, before I could consider a different tactic.

"No one is immune, and I'm not asking you to control, I'm asking you to influence her, nudge her into trusting you and realizing that returning to Nexa is in her best interest."

"If memory serves, you sent her off Nexa. Sold your own blood to slave traders."

"I entrusted my beloved granddaughter to worthy wardens. She needed to learn the reality of an infinite universe filled with infinite cruelty. She needed to learn that Nexa's methods are a benefit for everyone. Unfortunately, one of those wardens was not as attentive as he should have been, and we lost her for a time. Still, it wasn't a complete waste. She's no doubt learned some devastating lessons and with a little prompting, she could help us expand to other worlds."

"I convince her to return, and you leave all three of my children alone?" I asked, feeling sick.

"Well, that will be your first task," Megaera said with a grin too large, too cruel to ever be mistaken for the sincerity in her voice.

I sighed, knowing if I resisted, she would find another way to drag Phoenix home, but I would lose the only opportunity to save Athena. I knew how her twisted mind worked. She would kill Athena to show her displeasure, and move on to threatening my twins, or their father.

"I won't do anything that will endanger any of my daughters," I said finally.

It was a true statement, one that won her trust.

CHAPTER 4- SHARDS

"I'm ashamed to know you think of this girl as one of your own, truthfully," Megaera drawled.

"You refer to yourself as my grandmother, and we both know my biological grandmother was the Queen of Talaraine," I snapped. It was something I learned on Karabeeya, but I knew without doubt, Megaera had been aware of my actual heritage all along. She was the one who orchestrated my kidnapping as an infant so she could ensure her own son raised me, rather than my birth parents. I suspected it was my mother she really wanted to hurt. She was the daughter of a fling my grandfather had with the old Queen of Talaraine. I had never even met my biological mother, and I was confident she had no idea I was alive. Megaera was too skilled at tricking people into believing what she wanted them to.

Megaera stiffened. "While it's true your grandfather had a dalliance with the Talaraine tramp, you are more like me than you are like her or anyone else in your biological lineage. You have the potential to be extraordinary, as a true Deva." With that she snapped her fingers and Flunky walked into the room.

"Escort her to her new room, see that she is dressed appropriately," Megaera's eyes lingered on my arms as Flunky removed the shackles. They had once been covered with scars of her doing, but a healer had helped the skin remember how to heal correctly, and the scars were long since faded.

"I will speak with you again later," Megaera said sweetly. No matter her tone, I knew it was a threat.

I stood and followed Flunky quietly out of the room.

She silently took me to another floor, far from the prison, and opened the door to a room far larger than the one I grew up in. Did Megaera think a bribe of luxury would ease the fact that she was threatening Athena?

"I will stay with you," Flunky said placidly.

"Better idea," I snapped. "You leave now, and you have my word I will be dressed as the perfect Nexan Princess, or I throw you out of the room by force, snapping your neck if I have to, and then I will bar this room and dress as I see fit. I'm pretty good and modifying the uniform of a Nexan Princess, I've been doing it since I was six."

Either she heard the rumors about me, or she was a good enough empath to know I was telling the truth, because she wordlessly walked out of the room and shut behind her.

Naturally the door automatically locked, and I couldn't open it on my side, no matter how hard I forced the handle.

I huffed at their mistrust and looked around the room. There was a small bed in one corner, a table with a tray of food in the opposite corner, and a door between them to a decent bathroom, although it lacked everything, I had grown accustomed to on Karabeeya. The free wall had a wardrobe containing multiples of the same three outfits, all in the black and steel blue of the Royal House of Nexa.

I ate first, which was a mistake, the food was heavily seasoned, and Nexa imported their spices from other worlds. The result was spice in a way I had never experienced, and I immediately barfed it all back up. I then spent hours sitting next to the toilet, sipping nasty water until I no longer threw that up as well.

Then, I took a shower. The water was timed, another horrible thing I hated about this desert world, but at least it was hot. Unfortunately, I realized that sometime between my capture and now, likely while in that telepathic induced sleep, my wavy brown and white hair had matted. Worse, there was something gooey, rust brown, and difficult to remove in the mats. As soon as the water automatically shut off, I quickly dried and put on one of the uniforms from the closet. It consisted of a black sleeveless blouse and fitted tight skirt made of the same, stiff material. This was a uniform meant to be seen in, but not one that allowed for physical activity, and the shoes had an uncomfortable, high narrow heel. I didn't mind heels, I grew up in them, but I wasn't going to wear them until I had to leave the room.

I walked into the bathroom and tried to tame my hair, but it was a completely lost cause. With reluctance and resentment, I found a pair of scissors, no doubt left for this purpose, and carefully set to cutting the mats out of my hair and trimming it into something less embarrassing.

When I walked out of the bathroom again, I found that the food tray had been replaced without my knowledge while I cut my hair. The tray was filled with soft bland foods, including a heaping bowl of the mush I had been served in the cell. Because it wasn't enough to be in this fancier cell, Megaera wanted me to know that my every action was still being carefully monitored.

I had learned a rude gesture on Karabeeya, but it had originated on Talaraine, the planet of the 'Talaraine Tramp' I took the opportunity to do the gesture to each of the four corners of the room, so it would be seen by my watchers from at least one good angle.

With my left, non-dominant hand I flicked imaginary dirt from my thumbnail with my middle finger in a dismissive display. The gesture on Talaraine and Karabeeya, meant 'you are not worth the excrement I clean from my nails'. It was very rude, very gross, and slightly less deranged than screaming in an empty room.

My new ritual completed, I turned off the lights, enjoying the dark for the first time in who knew how long. Unfortunately, sleep did not come easily. I wanted to enter Betwixt, the Dream Realm only powerful Telepaths could willingly enter, so I could speak to Rowan. I missed my husband, and I needed to warn him of the danger to our children. Without the chemical in the air, I was lucid enough, but the bracelet cut off my power, and even if I didn't have the bracelet, it would have been a reckless attempt so close to Megaera and her clones. The impossibility of the wish did not make it less desirable.

I finally woke to the unexpected sound of my door unlocking. I clutched the scissors, but the door never opened. Finally, I climbed out of bed, forced myself to eat a *small* amount of food, and put the uncomfortable shoes on. I kept the scissors with me, slipping them in the waistband of my dress, although they were a poor weapon compared to what the guards carried.

There were no guards outside my door, no waiting clones. The hallway was empty, and as soon as I stepped into the hallway, I felt it, an impression brushing against the poor mental wall I built to protect myself from telepathy while I wore the bracelet.

It wasn't a command, or a subtle suggestion meant to influence my emotions. It was merely a request from a telepath less cruel than Megaera.

Because I knew I could ignore the request without compulsion to follow it, I obeyed it. This particular telepath had never tried to use his telepathy to control me, or as far as I knew, anyone else. Although there were a lot of other methods, he had no problem using.

I walked to the throne room. I was never once stopped or questioned. I couldn't bring myself to look at any of the others in the hallways, slaves running from errand to errand, government workers, or members of the Nexan Court. I didn't want to see what judgements lurked in their eyes, so I kept my gaze forward, on a part of the ceiling far down the hallway and walked with a purposeful trot that did not invite interruption.

When I reached the door to the throne room, I hesitated. I had not entered this room since my adopted mother, Millennia, was executed there. But the longer I stood outside the doors, the greater the chance that someone would observe my weakness. I pushed the door open and walked into an empty room.

I walked to the dais and sat on the bottom step, facing away from both the throne, and the spot on the floor where my mother had died. There was no stain there, of course, no flaw or mark to show where anyone died in this room. Fortunately, there had been enough death in this single room that neither Megaera nor any of her clones could enter it. It didn't fit with the Goddess of Life persona she maintained.

I didn't have to wait long before Prince Setne, my grandfather, walked into the room. We did not age quickly, so he looked at most in his early thirties, rather than over seventy, with brown-red hair cut in a short, severe style, and his own uniform as black and starched as mine.

"It's good to see you again." I waited until he was close enough for me to clearly see his eyes before I responded. My adopted father, Blaze, and my sister Phoenix didn't believe me, but I knew there were two sides of my grandfather. The kind man whose love and approval I craved as a child, and the cruel dictator who shot Millenia himself, and the way to tell which one I was dealing with was to look at his eyes. The more moss green specs in his rust brown eyes, the less cruel he was in that moment. If there were no green flecks, he was a monster.

Today his eyes were more green than brown, but I also knew that could change in an instant. Growing up, Phoenix thought I was insane for searching for a compassion she was convinced existed only as a farce.

Experiencing the nightmare of Megaera's telepathy personally, I wasn't so sure. The child in me wanted to believe that the more green in his eyes, the more I was seeing what he was really like, and the brown came when she controlled him, although no one believed he was one of her slaves.

"It's good to see you again," he said as he sat on the same step I did, about four feet away. He glanced at me, then looked down and started toying with the chain he kept under his shirt.

"I was told you were returned to us."

I smiled sadly, unwilling to say something snarky in that moment and risk aggravating him. Aggravation quickly turned kind Setne into cruel Setne.

"I was also told you have children. Twin daughters Thalia

and Calliope, and an older girl you adopted, Athena. When will they be joining us here?"

I shook my head. I could not stay silent on this. I would have to risk aggravating him. "Please, grandfather, let them grow up in their father's home."

"They would be better off here. The House of Deva must be reunited." He spoke with distracted agitation, as though reciting something that had been drilled into him repeatedly.

I looked him in the eye, relieved to see the green still there. "Do you truly believe that?" I risked. "Did you not send Juliet away from here, and ensure she never returned?"

He flinched when I said my mother's name.

"I didn't know you knew her name," he said finally, "But your children belong here. If you want them to stay on Karabeeya..." he flinched and closed his eyes tightly.

"Grandfather?" I whispered, knowing he was going to turn quickly.

"She wants to shift her focus to Talaraine, to scorch all life and memory from it, then use the husk of a planet to launch an attack on Karabeeya and do the same. Your children would be safer here."

He pulled the chain out from under his shirt, clenched it tightly and looked at me, with green eyes. "Without the dye and makeup, you look like Juliet," he whispered. He flinched and staggered to his feet, and fled, not through the main doors, but to a panel that led to an escape tunnel.

I followed, but stopped as the panel closed, catching it and keeping it open just a crack, I saw Setne collapse at Megaera's feet.

"He's getting more difficult to control," she seethed to her companion. "I should have never brought the girl back."

My breath hitched as I quietly removed my shoes and walked out the opposite door as Setne was dragged through the tunnel.

CHAPTER 5- MANIPULATION

I returned to my room and curled up on the bed under the thin blanket. If I was lucky, my watchers would think I was asleep. I hoped they wouldn't see me cry.

I didn't get to grieve before Flunky walked into the room.

"You are to leave now, to retrieve your sister," Flunky commanded.

I took a slow breath. "I'm not going anywhere," I said. My voice was husky. I cringed. There was too much risk in Megaera learning I had witnessed her regaining control of her slave, my grandfather.

"Not even for Athena?" Flunky asked cruelly.

I wiped my eyes, and climbed out of the bed. I kept my head down as I shoved my shoes back on. "Ready whenever you are," I hissed.

"Follow me," Flunky ordered.

I walked out of the room, following Flunky has I quickly wiped my face. This was faster than I anticipated, but as I walked, I realized that I couldn't bring Phoenix back here. What if it simply took more time for Megaera to control Phoenix than it did for her to control me?

Flunky led me to the hangar, where I was instructed to climb into the nearest ship. As I walked up the ramp, I realized I wouldn't see my grandfather again, and that was likely the real reason I was being sent after Phoenix so quickly.

"Give me your wrist," Flunky ordered.

I held out my hand, and she efficiently removed the bracelet. I felt my power return with a surge of energy, and the first thing I did was strengthen my mental wall.

To my relief, the pilot was an ordinary citizen, and we were the only two people on the ship. Flunky did not come, and a quick check confirmed the pilot lacked any telepathic ability.

I settled in a small bunk in a tiny room. As soon as we were out of the atmosphere, I settled into a true deep sleep.

Getting to the Betwixt was a feat only a few telepaths were capable of, but it was something I had experience in. As soon as I began to dream, I used my telepathy to shift the dream, going deeper until the dream shifted into a beautiful garden my husband and I created back when I was pregnant with the twins, bedridden, and desperate for some kind of diversion.

The garden was secure, our own personal haven that no other uninvited telepath could enter. There was still some risk, if Megaera was in an unsecured part of the Betwixt, she could sense my presence, but she wouldn't be able to find me or know what I was doing. However, while I was out of her range in the waking world, she wouldn't know I entered the Betwixt, making it unlikely she would know to look for me.

The flowers in the garden were big, some blooms were nearly as tall as I was, and a few had centers that glowed faintly, creating a multicolored light source that lit the entire garden. I sat on my favorite bench, a plush one that had the perfect balance of support and softness and waited.

And waited.

And waited.

And was jarred awake by the chimes of the intercom system. The pilot oh so helpfully wanted to update his only passenger on the status of the journey. I cursed the pilot silently and laid down again.

Unfortunately, I couldn't fall back asleep. Without knowing

Rowan's sleep schedule, I wasn't sure waiting was even the best option. I would need to leave a message in the Betwixt, something I wasn't currently capable of. Messages, like the plants in the garden, would require manipulating a part of the Betwixt into a permanent form fitting my purpose. I would need to build up my strength before I attempted it.

Sullen, I stayed on the cot until the ship landed, the engines completely shut down, and the pilot nervously came looking for me.

"Your Highness, we have arrived," the pilot said timidly.

It occurred to me that this pilot likely had orders to see me off the ship, while at the same time, he lacked the authority to command a member of the Nexan Royal Family.

Since I had no qualms with him, I left the room and walked off the ship. I had to blink several times as my eyes burned from the bright sunlight, a harsh change after my time underground on Nexa.

It took only a moment to identify my new minder. A telepath, one stronger than me, and concerningly, impossibly, stronger than Megaera, stood waiting with mercenaries. He was a tall man, taller than me, taller than Rowan, with pure white hair. We Nexans were powerful, magically gifted, but when our minds were overpowered by a telepath, the world knew it by the thin streak of white that appeared in our hair, mine had several streaks. However, if a puppet willingly gave up their freedom, often to gain more power or aid their master in some shared goal, their hair turned pure white, demonstrating they were the perfect puppet.

I knew to fear anyone with pure white hair, and I had never seen it on so powerful a telepath.

"Greetings to you, Princess Hope, I am Kale. I will be assisting you on your mission," he said.

I gave him my most flirtatious smile, even as I shored up my mental walls so he would be able to sense nothing at all. Hopefully, he would think me nothing more than a power-hungry flirt.

"How will you assist me?" I asked, glancing at his followers.

"I will personally retrieve your errant sister." He held out a whip to me. It wasn't new, the frayed cords had dry blood on them, and the handle was well worn.

I glanced at the whip, uncomfortable.

"While I retrieve your errant sister, I will need you to oversee the workers here."

"You use a whip?" I asked, uneasy. Megaera didn't use a physical method of persuasion to control her slaves, and this man was stronger than her, it shouldn't have been necessary. "Not telepathic control?"

"I use both," he said easily. "But I find a tangible reminder reinforces the obedience more quickly. There are three slaves I need you to monitor. Don't worry about causing excessive harm, there is a healer strong enough to heal any injury, including his own."

I clenched my jaw at his cavalier attitude toward healers. Healing was exhausting, more so when a healer healed their own injuries, and if someone healed themselves constantly, there was a risk of the experience growing more painful with each subsequent healing, which could eventually cause a nervous breakdown.

"Princess Hope, you will need the whip to keep your new charges in line," Kale pressed. "I have been told you lack the skill to control slaves telepathically."

Reluctantly, I accepted the whip, hoping I wouldn't have to use it. I knew I would be doing terrible things to protect my family, but this was not what I had in mind.

"How long am I watching them? What am I watching them do?" I bit back my next question. Why was he entrusting me with this task?

Kale smiled at me, and I grinned back, even as his expression made me want to back away and maybe throw the whip at his face after charging it with explosive magic.

"Walk with me, Princess Hope."

I fell into step next to Kale as he walked away from the ship, and the mercenaries.

"Are you familiar with the legends of the original Novem?" Kale asked without preamble.

I scrunched my nose. "I know enough to know every planet and culture has a different version of the legends."

Kale nodded. "Have you heard of the crystal weapons?"

I shook my head.

"It is said that before the gods withdrew from our universe, they gifted their demigod children, the original Novem, with crystal weapons from the Divine Realm."

I barely managed to avoid rolling my eyes. I did know that story. Supposedly the Gods gave mystic weapons to their children, then gave a portion of their power to the grandchildren most like them. The weapons could only be used by the reincarnations of the original Novem, while the power given to those chosen grandchildren was passed from worthy vessel to worthy vessel, ensuring there were always living Gods among us. That story was part of Megaera's propaganda to convince the people of Nexa to worship her as one of the living gods.

"These crystal weapons have been lost to us, some shattered, some hidden and forgotten. I believe the twin fans of the Dreamer are located in on these catacombs. You are to ensure my slaves search them daily, and do not shirk their duties. This is a task given to me by my master, the Utopian.

"The mercenaries will guard the entrance to the catacombs. They are a superstitious group who are reluctant to enter the catacombs. Will you be able to handle three slaves on your own?"

I scoffed and gave him my best offended stink eye. "I don't need help watching a few slaves. Although it surprises me that you would hire cowards too afraid to enter catacombs."

"Their superstitious natures can be molded to my advantage."

We climbed a grassy hill parallel to a forest, and at the crest of the hill, a large, opulent mansion came into view.

EPISODE 6 THE BROKEN MANSION

As we approached the mansion, a few things became apparent. First, there was a waterfall on the side of the building. It originated from a grate on the top floor and flowed into a pond on the side of the building. As I studied this feature, I wondered if the water leaked from the pond into the mansion, because while the building was impressive from a distance, as we approached it, I could see the way the gold leafing was peeling off the walls and when we walked inside there was a thick layer of dust that covered everything, with clear paths where the residents often walked. It was an Amaranthian style manor, I could tell by the lift in the center of the building, a platform that had no rail or walls and would rise and lower, taking the rider to whatever level of the manor they wanted.

I chewed my lip as I looked at the lift. Was it possible we were in the Amaranth Empire?

Kale had no interest in giving me any kind of tour, he merely took me to the room I was assigned and left me there with instructions to meet the slaves outside the front doors in the morning.

I glanced around and laid on the bed. It took longer than I wanted to fall asleep, and longer than I expected to enter the Betwixt.

I had hoped expending energy to go into the Betwixt again would have a better result than conserving it to later create a message, but once again Rowan wasn't there.

I woke up tired and cranky, forced myself to wear the restrictive uniform of a Nexan princess. The black material was depressing. On Karabeeya, I had developed a fondness for pink and only wore black as an accent color. Being back in the color made me sick, and it aggravated me enough that I was almost to the door before I realized I left that stupid whip in the room and I had to go back for it.

Since the time I was given was 'morning' I did not consider myself late when I left the building and approached three haggard men. The eldest was a stern looking man with black hair streaked with white. He watched me with unexpected frankness. The man next to him was slightly shorter than me, with downcast eyes and hair like a rung out filthy mophead perched on his head.

Then there was the third man.

Freakishly tall with lanky limbs and hair more white than black. His fear and self-loathing collided with my mental wall, as though desperate for me to share his pain. I recoiled and hastily shored up my wall. Once, when I was a little girl, my grandmother forced me to watch as she finished breaking down one of her victims, and he willingly gave her his free will to tamper with as she saw fit. This man was on the cusp of breaking down and making the same choice, if he didn't end his own life first. I thinned my wall enough to feel the self-loathing again and pushed it to the side so I could examine the telepathic suggestions implanted. Subconscious suggestions that could influence behavior and emotion if the victim wasn't aware of them.

I loosened some of the suggestions, so they would be easier to ignore. It would take time to remove them completely, but I couldn't quite risk it, already the stern man was glaring suspiciously at me.

"My name is Hope, I will be watching you today," I said, managing a small smile. I held the whip loosely at my side, wishing I could just drop it. The only thing that stopped me was the possibility of some kind of surveillance.

"What are your names?" I said when they stayed silent.

"Why do you care?" Mop Top surprised me by asking.

I shrugged. "It's demeaning not to know."

"Yue," the stern man said. "This is my brother Taichi, Tai for short, and the healer is Tori."

I looked from Yue to Tai. There was some passing resemblance, but I would not have guessed they were siblings, partially because the resemblance was not that strong, and partially because it was rare for slavers to allow siblings to stay together.

I suspected Kale was using the threat of harming Yue to break Tai down further.

"Well, Yue," I identified him as the leader easily. "Do you know the way to the catacombs?" I asked.

"We all do," Yue confirmed.

"Great, I don't, so please lead the way."

CHAPTER 7 – TELEPATHS AND PRISONERS

Tai smirked, then quickly schooled his expression back into one of beaten compliance when he noticed I was looking at him.

Yue led the way into the woods. It wasn't really a forest so much as an overgrown orchard. I could still see where the oldest trees grew in straight lines, but younger trees grew in randomly, the result of fruit dropping from the tree and sprouting into new trees, and fruit being moved as animals consumed it and dropped the seeds elsewhere.

The orchard sat against a true forest, but the entrance to the catacombs was at the edge of the orchard. It was little more than a carved-out cave entrance, notable only because the entrance was guarded by two cranky mercenaries.

As I passed the mercenaries, I thinned my mental wall just enough to know that there were no others inside the catacombs. Once we were away from the mercenaries, we would be alone.

Yue did not slow down his pace. Each man grabbed a lantern from where they had been stashed near the entrance and continued in. I followed, but it didn't take long before I was hopelessly lost. If they chose to leave me down in these tunnels, I could wander for days and never finds my way out.

"Katsu, Tori, continue where we left off yesterday," Yue said.

Tai glanced at his brother, then me, before he wordlessly followed Tori down the tunnel.

"You have something to say?" I asked as soon as they were gone.

"You're not a slaver," Yue said firmly.

I felt the familiar brush against my mental wall, the warning that a powerful telepath was attempting to snoop. It should not have been possible for Yue to be able to test my mental wall. While not all slavers restricted the power of their slaves, Kale at least should have been smart enough to do so. Instead, it seemed he only limited the power of the healer, no doubt to ensure his victims lived, but stayed weak and in pain.

"You're a telepath," I remarked, careful to keep my tone light.

"It's a little-known fact to outsiders, but telepathy is fairly common among dragons."

"You didn't hesitate to share your little-known fact with me, and I'm a Novem from Nexa," I said carefully. While Megaera knew about my family, I didn't want to advertise that I was married to a dragon. Any references to my husband and daughters needed to be carefully avoided, or I risked drawing unwanted attention to them beyond what there already was. The Utopian was the shadowy benefactor of Nexa. The alliance between him and Megaera gave Nexa the military strength to oppose the Amaranth Empire. I didn't know how close the two truly were and couldn't risk giving Kale's master more information than he already knew.

"Let's keep this simple and not lie," Yue said with a slight laugh. "You are Talarainian, not Nexan."

"I'm a quarter Nexan," I said quickly. I was also only a quarter Talarainian, and unsure of why he focused on that particular planet in my ancestry.

"You are also at least a mage, although I would guess you are more likely an enchantress."

I sneered at that assessment. Amara, the self-proclaimed goddess of love, had once told me that on Karabeeya, and Nexa, the Novem gods and goddesses were called enchanters and enchantresses. I would not even respond to the delusional claim that I might be mistaken for some make believe deity.

"Look, I'm going to guess you don't want to be on this planet any more than I do," Yue began.

"Great guess," I hissed.

"So, let's make a deal," he said quickly, jumping on my sarcasm as though it were agreement. "Help me, and as soon as I'm back on Talaraine, I can help you with whatever mess you are caught in. I have connections, and considerable resources. As soon as I can access them, I can personally ensure your safety, and the safety of anyone else caught up in whatever they have on you."

I chewed my lip. It was said that the Nexan Novem could always know truth from lie, but that wasn't quite accurate. It was more like the telepaths in my family were really good at knowing if someone was sincere. Yue could believe everything he said, but it didn't make it fact.

On the other hand, *I* had considerable connections on Talaraine. My mother was the Queen of the entire planet. Granted, there was that small matter of her believing I had been murdered as an infant, but maybe Yue had the connections to contact her, and convince her to contact Rowan and Prince Remy.

"Aren't you loyal to Kale?" I asked. This conversation could just be an elaborate trap. Kale struck me as the type of sadistic monster who would set up something like this just for his own entertainment.

Yue shook his head. "I have no loyalty to Kale, and thanks to some training I received from an old friend when we were children, I was able to eventually resist Kale's control and even those sly telepathic suggestions."

"I would like to verify that," I said. I sat down on the cold, filthy floor.

Yue shrugged and sat down across from me. I shifted until I was comfortable and placed my hand on his right temple. The physical touch made this slightly easier, although entering another's thoughts and subconscious and being able to shift through and alter them was my absolute least favorite aspect of my telepathy.

Yue probably agreed thinking I was going to view his memories, but it was deeper than that. Like Kale and Megaera, I could alter the subconscious, implant suggestions that could alter a victim's behavior, personality, or temperament. It wasn't full control, although I could probably do that too. Full control of a puppet wasn't something I had or would ever try.

He had a strong mental wall, but the moment he lowered it to let me see his memories, I had access to everything.

I searched through his subconscious quickly. He had a fear of small animals, a crushing fear of losing his brother, and a weakness for sweets. It was enough to tell me what was him, and what was the two orders another telepath had implanted.

To Yue's credit, these were strong, difficult to place, and too well buried for me to remove in a single setting, or even in the course of the few days it would take before Kale returned.

"You have a subconscious order preventing you from leaving," I said.

"But there isn't one that would compel me to trick or betray you." Yue paused and pulled away. "If you are strong enough to find the commands I couldn't break down, you are strong enough to enter the Dream Realm."

"With risk," I scooted away from him. The only advantage of being able to deep dive into someone's mind, their motivations and personality, was I had a strong grasp on his trustworthiness.

"Could you get a message to Kahlan Perihelion on Talaraine?"

I shrugged. "I'll try. I haven't been able to reach my allies. Our sleep schedule is off track."

"Have you tried entering the Dream Realm in midmorning?"

I shook my head. "You might have the strength to resist Kale, but your brother does not. If he sees me sleeping rather than watching over all of you like I should, he'll be forced to report it."

"He won't come this way until it's time to return to the mansion." Yue stood. "I know a place where you would be more comfortable."

I followed him down another tunnel, to a room, a shrine really, with an elaborate coffin in the center. The floor was elaborately carved, possibly the most uncomfortable floor in the catacombs.

"The top of the coffin is smooth and flat," Yue said. "I keep a bag on the other side with food, medical supplies, and a few other things that are critical. If something happens to me, make sure that bag reaches an ally."

"Of you or me?" I asked with a snort.

"An enemy of the Utopian will suffice. Do you need help climbing up on the stone slab?"

I winced, not thrilled with the idea of lying on a stone coffin, deep underground with countless other corpses. Without a better suggestion, I climbed onto the coffin and laid down. Yue stood over me. If he had a knife in his hand, it would complete the image of being sacrificed on an altar.

I winked at Yue, then settled against the cold stone and took slow, deep breaths until I entered a meditative state and slipped into the realm of telepaths and prisoners.

This time when I entered the garden, I wasn't alone, but neither was Rowan.

CHAPTER 8 BETWIXT

I tensed, but did not immediately lash out at Amara, which was excellent restraint considering she believed the same nonsense that Megaera used to keep the populace of Nexa enslaved to her will. That she, like Megaera, wanted me to play in the same delusion.

"Hope, I am only here to offer aid," Amara said quickly.

I snarled at her, then turned my full attention to Rowan. He was looking over my shoulder, his gaze unfocused.

"The curse of the colalace crystal extends to the dream realm?" I whispered.

"The blindness is complete, no matter the realm," he said gently. He reached out, and I rushed into his arms. The Betwixt may have been the realm of dreams, but here, in this moment, he felt warm, real. I could feel the way his hands trembled as he held me, I could smell the faint aroma of his cologne.

"Are you hurt?" he whispered.

I shook my head and buried my face in the nape of his neck. "You healed me with a broken colalace crystal, my injuries healed, but you won't ever see again." I pulled away and studied his eyes. They were still clear, still the rich blue I adored, but the pupil was too small, and the gaze never met mine.

He smiled faintly, the skin around his eyes crinkled. "It's a miniscule loss if it means I can still hear your voice, and hold you," he ran his fingers through my hair. As his fingers trailed across my face I grabbed his hand, clasping it tightly and keeping him from feeling the tears that rolled down my face.

Yue would wake me, possibly any moment, and the time for grief would have to come later. I released Rowan's hand, put my hand gently on his neck, and rested my forehead against his.

Telepaths like Rowan and me guarded our minds, careful to never reveal too much, or allow a dark telepath access to influence us. However, Rowan and I were soulmates, bound by our trust and love, and when needed, we could open our minds to each other and expose our every thought and memory to each other. It was difficult, even with my soulmate, to allow such intimacy. It was also the fastest way to share information.

Rowan sensed me remove my mental wall, and immediately removed his. Through our seamless communication, Rowan learned of Yue's request, and the threat to our children. I learned of his fear after my disappearance, and his desperation to regain the independence he lost when he lost his sight. He had told me the truth, he would have sacrificed anything to save my life, but it didn't mean that sacrifice was easy, or he didn't struggle. His frustration and wounded pride caused him to struggle to focus and he needed Amara to anchor him so he could remain in the Betwixt for an extended period of time.

He nudged the focus of our bond to his memories of our children. He showed me what he saw when I first held the twins, then when I helped Athena with her homework for the first time. We could have stayed like that forever, but I felt Rowan's fatigue and reluctantly severed the bond.

"You've been here too long, even with Amara's help," I whispered.

He shook his head, but the denial was reflexive. He knew he couldn't fool me.

"Thank you, for your help," I said, facing Amara.

"I have two gifts for you," she said. She motioned gracefully to the bench next to her, and a slender, canine creature jumped onto the bench. "Her name is Dina, and she will take messages through the Betwixt for you, so you and Rowan can communicate without having to sync your sleep schedule." She took a red shard of glass out of her pocket. "This has two functions. If you rub it, it will call Dina to you. It will also show you the Aura of someone who has a soulmate."

"Why would the second function be remotely helpful?" I asked, scrunching my nose as I accepted the red shard.

"There is power in knowing who someone loves." Amara said cryptically as she faded away.

I leaned back against Rowan. "I don't think Megaera would have just one way of reaching the girls."

"No, once I'm completely certain our children are safe, I will let you know. I have the other half of the shard that will call Dina."

"I'll keep playing along with Megaera's demands, but I don't want it to be too easy for her."

"I'll reach out to this Kahlan," Rowan promised.

I rested against him and closed my eyes, reluctantly allowing the Betwixt to fade away.

CHAPTER 9 – CHAOS SPRITE

When I opened my eyes, I was back in the catacombs, laying on the creepy stone coffin, and this time, Dina was with me.

"That's a chaos sprite!" Yue yelped.

"I made a new friend in the Betwixt," I said, glaring at the creature. Amara had left out the part where Dina was called a chaos sprite.

Dina jumped onto the coffin, licked my face with her hot, rough tongue, then vanished.

"Those things are anarchy wrapped in a deceptively adorable façade," Yue grumbled.

"I got that when you called her a chaos sprite," I said as I climbed off the coffin. "She's going to be my messenger. We're getting help."

Yue smiled. As my words sank in, his shoulders relaxed. "I guess I better start searching the catacombs, that way, I can honestly say I searched while Kale was gone."

I watched Yue, Tai, and Tori for three boring days before Kale returned to the compound. His return was marked by a message for the three to go with the mercenaries to build some wood structure near the pool of water adjacent to the mansion.

I wasn't expected to do anything, so I hid in my room, and used the red glass for the first time.

I rubbed the glass between my hands enthusiastically and felt the shard warm with the friction.

Dina appeared, rubbed her head against my left knee, then she jumped on my bed.

"Hey," I objected as white hair settled on the blanket as she curled up in a tight ball.

"I like this bed, it's comfortable," Dina said sullenly.

I gaped at the chaos sprite. "I don't know why, but I assumed you couldn't talk."

"What an absurd assumption. Why did you summon me? Was it to learn what all I am capable of?"

I paused. Since she brought it up, it did sound like an intriguing lesson, but there were other priorities, higher priorities.

"Phoenix is arriving today."

"That's fortunate timing. Your lover has arranged a rescue with some interesting people on Talaraine. The rescue should be able to easily accommodate your sister, although there won't be time to get the message to the rescuers."

"That's actually better. If the rescuers are caught, they won't know I wanted them to rescue Phoenix as well, and they won't be able to share what they don't know with a telepathic interrogator."

"Exactly. Your lover never told Kahlan about Phoenix. This was all set up under the guise of rescuing Yue. If your sister missed this recue, something Rowan feared was likely, another would have been set up with another excuse. You'll need to arrange for all who need rescuing to be in the orchard."

"Can I go with them?" I asked.

Dina's head drooped. "The children aren't safe yet."

I nodded, resigned to the fact that I would need to continue being Megaera's unwilling pawn until they were safe. "I can play the part of livid sister who lost her prize when Phoenix escapes."

"Good, since that is settled, I will deliver your message. It's nearly noon where your children live, and Athena always has a snack for me."

"Excellent priority," I deadpanned.

"I always prioritize food," Dina said. The next instant, she was gone.

Left alone, I had two choices, I could go out and be observed, or I could hide in my room a little longer.

Naturally I started exploring my room. I found a small box tucked under the bed in the far corner. The box was covered in a thick layer of dust and grime, and it took some work to pry it open, but once I did, I was not completely disappointed.

I had hoped for a weapon, but the box was filled instead with tarnished jewelry and shredded strips of bright fabric.

I didn't care about the jewelry, but the fabric had potential. I sat down and methodically wrapped each strand around my forearms, creating festive faux bracers. I kept the pink deliberately close to my wrists.

The goal was for Phoenix to notice this deviation from my uniform, and once she was safe, hopefully she would realize the ribbons were a message.

I was no longer loyal to Nexa.

CHAPTER 10 – THE HISTORY OF THE SISTERS

I just managed to tie the last ribbon on my arm before one of the mercenaries pounded on my door.

"Kale will arrive soon. He wants you to wait in the garden on the top floor. I will escort you there."

"Lucky me, lead the way," I hissed. I gave him a smile, but judging from his reaction, it was an ineffective one at best.

He took me to the top floor of the compound, a huge, open space that had been converted into an indoor garden, complete with a large fountain that fed water into a stream that fed the waterfall down the side of the building.

I walked to the windows and looked down at the pond where Yue, Tai, and Tori were building something. Yue looked up, and I followed his gaze to a small ship landing on the field. Unlike the landing yard, the field's grass had been healthy before the ship landed, and I knew the grass was going to be scorched where the ship touched it.

The ship settled, and eventually Kale walked off the ship. He was followed by a reluctant Phoenix.

I leaned my forehead against the glass. I hadn't seen my little sister in four years, and at eighteen, she was not any taller, but her face had changed a little, and her hair was a matted mess that fell nearly to her feet in a disgusting braid.

Phoenix fixated on the grass, then the sky, her eyes wide and her expression of wonder visible even from my vantage point. Kale noticed her wandering attention and stuck her with enough force to knock her to the ground.

I tensed, feeling the energy of my magic shift in my fist before I forced it to dissipate. I didn't know Kale's range and couldn't risk him reading emotions I wasn't adequately containing within my mental wall.

The blow didn't seem to cause real damage, Phoenix climbed back to her feet, and resumed walking respectfully behind Kale, although I noticed she showed Tai as much interest as she had shown the sky. I knew that immediate interest, of one telepath recognizing their compatible equal. If they escaped together, it would give my sister the chance to experience the kind of love I shared with Rowan.

As soon as she was on the lift, I used the faintest strands of telepathy. Her wall was more like chain mail, with tiny cracks. I used those cracks when we were children to better understand her emotions and how to convince her to not do something stupid. Now, I used those cracks to carefully shift and taint her emotions. It required more finesse than I normally needed, but if she realized what I was doing, she could use her own power to block me. Phoenix was the stronger telepath, but our father, or rather her father and my adopted father, sealed her power to protect her from Megaera. I had always resented the fact that he protected only her from Megaera, and I threaded that resentment into her.

She didn't see me immediately, but she was all I could focus on. This close, I could see, and smell, that she hadn't bathed in who knew how long, and her skin was streaked with rashes and acne.

When she saw me, her expression darkened, and she took a

small step back. "I should have known."

It hurt, but it was the plan, what had to happen if I had any hope of protecting my sister, and my children.

"I'll be right back, one of my slaves was apparently out of line in my absence," Kale said.

I tried not to flinch as my stomach clenched. There was nothing negative to report, Yue had assured me that they had not stepped out of line, careful not to raise anyone's ire. Which meant that he simply wanted to break Tai down further.

"Yes, darling, you go deal with that," I said, flicking my wrist dismissively at him. I could act, I could do this, for my daughters.

"Are you mocking me?" Phoenix demanded as she glared at the colorful strips of cloth that covered my arms.

Belatedly, I saw what I should have noticed first. Her arms were marred with long thin scars, not unlike those on Tai, Yue, and Tori. It was common, to punish slaves by slashing their arms with thin blades, proof of their disobedience and reminders that rebellious acts were always brutally punished.

"Oh please," I scoffed. "Jealousy doesn't become you. Do you have any idea how hard it's been to track you down?" Let her think that's what I've been up to the past four years. It was nearly as bad as the truth. I had pretended she had escaped and was living somewhere safe. It was a fantasy I created so I could justify living on Karabeeya with my family instead of searching for her.

"Aww, poor Hope! Did I inconvenience you?" she asked with a snark that was so much like her response to our childish arguments, I couldn't help but give her a genuine smirk.

I used telepathy to feed her anger, her hatred, just a little. I had to make sure she refused my offer, while ensuring it looked like I truly tried.

"Hmm, you look like hell," I commented, slowly approaching her. It was so hard to see her like this, a hardened girl, barely an adult, who had suffered so much.

She glared at me like I was sludge on her shoe, until a scream cut through the room, originating at the base of the waterfall. I could use it to aggravate Phoenix.

"Ignore it," I said with a flippant smirk.

"Yeah," she snapped. "Ignore other people's pain. That's something you excel at."

I blinked. I had apparently fed into hatred that was already there.

Of course, she hated me for what I did to Kayda, it was unforgiveable.

"Our father called in a favor from the Utopian to track you down. Do you have any idea what that cost?"

"All of Nexa?" Phoenix asked with a perky smile.

"Not that high a price."

Nervously, I thrust my hands in my pockets and found the crystal Amara gave me. On impulse, I took it out and looked at Phoenix through the crystal. Her aura was a haze of color that shifted over her skin. Phoenix was a telepath, but she also had cyrokinesis, her magic allowed her to easily cool and freeze things. I could see that cold, light blue magic shift around her protectively, along with the gold of her telepathy, tainted by our father's seal.

There was also something else, an orange fire magic dancing with the ice magic, and a yellow telepathic magic that was eating at the seal, freeing her power.

"That's new," I murmured.

"Are you taking me back?" Phoenix demanded.

Curious, I walked to the window, where I had a clear view of Kale whipping Tai I used the crystal to look at them. Tai's magic was fire, yellow telepathy, and the thinnest tendrils of ice. I couldn't identify Kale's magic, but it looked tainted, and there were colors dancing, causing me to wonder if this monster had a soulmate, and if that soulmate knew he was some telepath's broken slave.

"Kale is a trusted friend of the Utopian," I said, still studying him. "He has agreed to the initial agreement Scale broke when he sold you."

In the window's reflection, I saw Phoenix tense and roll her shoulders. I turned to face her, worried about the naked fear on her face, a response she didn't have when she thought I was going to take her back to Nexa.

"Phoenix, just tell me you'll fall in line. I'll vouch for you," I said quietly, wishing now that I had just done what Megaera wanted. If this place was worse than Nexa, maybe it would have been better to try and mount a rescue on Nexa, rather than risk one failing here.

"And the second I step off that line, we'll both be punished," Phoenix said bitterly.

"The solution is simple, don't step off that line," I said automatically.

"I'm not you," she spat.

Keeping up with this role was too difficult. I clenched my hand in a tight fist at my side. No, Phoenix wasn't me. She had never made my mistakes. She didn't abandon her sister to monsters and pretend it was fine because Phoenix might have had the opportunity to escape... eventually. She didn't hurt people at Megaera's command. She had never hurt anyone with anything other than words.

The lift descended, then rose, bring a blood splattered Kale, holding his blood-soaked whip into the room. The moment Phoenix saw him, she stepped to the side and her gaze returned to the floor.

I kept my gaze off that bloody whip. "There's no need to interrogate her today," I managed with an indifference I didn't feel. "She's refusing to come back." I paused, preparing myself for how to convince him to keep her with Tai and the others, when he interrupted me.

"It's already set up. I want to know the extent of her telepathy."

"She's an empath," I said flatly. Empaths were the weakest of the telepaths, everyone knew that. With the seal on her power, there was no way he could learn any different. I glanced at her, although without the shard, I could no longer see the fire magic eating away the seal on her power.

"I'm curious."

Something in his tone scared me. I walked to the window and looked down. Tai was slumped on the wood frame he had been tied to, but now he was under the waterfall.

It was likely Megaera already told him about her power, or she did something stupid on the way here that revealed she had cyrokinesis. I could use this to my advantage, lessen any suspicion he had about me, while at the same time, create an opening for the rescue.

"Uh," I took a deep breath. "She's got cyrokinesis. Get her to waste her magic first, then leave her and those other slaves all outside for the night, by tomorrow morning she'll be so exhausted from the drain and trying to protect her new friends, it will be easy to get a full read of her abilities. You have enough security for that, I presume?"

"Easily," Kale said with a slow grin.

"Then I'll be back next week," I glanced at Phoenix. "Maybe a week under your supervision will change her mind." I walked to the lift. If this rescue didn't work, I couldn't spend a week hiding in my room, but the implication would give me time to think of something else.

As I rode the lift down, I saw Kale brandish the whip, and Phoenix flinch away from it.

CHAPTER 11 – PUNISHMENT

I hurried to my room, filled with self-loathing, and curled in my bed. It was hours before I fell asleep, and when I woke, it was to the smell of smoke and the heat of fire. I climbed out of my window, suspecting that I wouldn't be able to leave through the door, and ran from the building. I turned once and saw flames that danced over the roof of the building. I could hear the screams and explosions of a battle.

This was my chance to get away, without Megaera realizing I betrayed her. I ran to the woods, forming a plan. I could hide in the catacombs, then use the crystal to send a message to Rowan. He could rescue me, it would probably be easier than this rescue, and I could hide until our children were safe, then rejoin my family.

I took a few steps into the orchard, and my head exploded with pain. I lost my balance and fell to the ground. The pressure of the dirt against my face was unbearable as the pain focused on that sensation. I wanted to move, but a slight shift told me it was impossible.

"My darling granddaughter," Megaera cooed. "Did you just run from an attack?"

There was no way to answer her, not with the pain, but

I doubted she wanted a genuine answer anyway. Even with the pain, I could sense her rage, even if I couldn't see her.

"You know, little princess, I came here to ensure you followed the simple order I gave you. I was eager to be reunited with my granddaughters. Instead, I arrive to find your sister gone, the mansion on fire, and you running away like some common coward. Did you even use your power to convince your sister to return to your family?"

"Not yet, she's too strong," I whispered.

"The next time you fail me, I will administer this same punishment to the oldest girl," Megaera sighed. "Your precious Athena."

Her hands grabbed my head, palms cupped over my ears. The pain that raged through my ears, then through my throat, and back through my head chased, away the mild annoyance of her initial telepathic attack.

I think I screamed, but it was impossible to hear anything, not when the pain consumed all. I wasn't even sure when she let me go, or how long I laid in the dirt, howling soundlessly.

Eventually I woke, although I had no recollection of falling asleep. The pain was gone, blessedly, except for a raw soreness in my throat. I rolled onto my back and realized I had made no sound at all with the motion. I coughed, and still there was no sound.

Nervously, I brought my hands together in a firm clap, and there was still nothing. Reluctantly, I felt my ears, and felt the clotted blood that still seeped slowly into my hair.

How ironic. I had taken my husband's sight, and now Megaera had taken my hearing completely.

There would be time to mourn the loss later, I knew I couldn't keep lying on the ground. If Megaera had to come get me, the punishment would be far worse.

I climbed to my feet and walked back to the mansion. The building was burned nearly to the ground, with only two partial walls remaining. There was also no one in the area. I turned around. This made no sense. Had something happened to everyone? Was this another trap? What reason could Megaera possibly have for leaving me alone after destroying my hearing in retaliation for running away?

I walked back to the catacombs. As I walked through the overgrown orchard, I realized it made no sense to punish me for trying to run, then leave me on the planet. It was more likely that they still thought I was unconscious in the orchard while they took care of some other situation. The more I considered it, the more I was forced to acknowledge that they would be back for me, but at the very least, I could get the medical supplies from the pack Yue stashed there.

I grabbed the bag, then sat down on the coffin slab. I began to quickly look through it.

The food in the bag was barely edible, the medical supplies barely enough to clean up the blood on my face and neck. I suspected the real value was at the bottom of the bag, an ebony box wrapped in smelly rags.

The box contained a beautiful fan, light blue, and made entirely from crystal. I had heard of fans like this one, equal parts ornament and weapon. It was heavy enough to bludgeon someone, and thick enough to serve as a shield. Next to the fan, there was a knife made from the same light blue crystal, encased in a sheath made of black stone, inlaid with the same blue crystal. I picked it up, took it out of the sheath, and held it with a smile. It was perfectly balanced, and the exact length I preferred in a small blade. I sheathed the blade and took the third item out of the box. It was a necklace, with a pink crystal shard as the pendant. Despite the different color, the pink stone looked like it might have been the same type of crystal as the blade and the fan.

I carefully packed everything back up and took the shard out of my pocket.

"Dina." I said.

In seconds, Dina appeared on top of the coffin.

Her mouth moved, but I probably lacked the ability to read the lips of a human, let alone a chaos sprite.

"I can't hear," I said. "Megaera is here, and she probably still thinks I'm unconscious, so I don't have a lot of time. Can you communicate with me telepathically?"

Slowly, Dina shook her head.

"Hmm, well, that sucks. Can you write?"

Again, Dina shook her head.

"Yes or no questions it is then. Are my children safe yet?"

Dina shook her head.

I sighed. "Then I guess I better go find Kale or Megaera and be a good little puppet. Can you take this box to Rowan?"

Dina nodded and I set the box in front of her.

"Take it now, before Kale sees it, I think this is something he's been looking for. You can see if Athena has a snack waiting for you."

Dina gave a slow, deliberate nod, then vanished with the box.

I slung the bag over my shoulder, so I had a likely excuse for my absence, and slowly trudged back to the ruins of the mansion. This time, Kale was waiting next to his ship. He approached me and held a slate up to my face. I took a step back and read what he wrote.

~If you are done wandering the woods, we are going after the escaped slaves. You are to find your traitor of a sister, and I will get Taichi Equinox back. ~

I scowled at Kale. If he already knew I had lost my hearing, he likely knew I wasn't a willing pawn in this sick game. It would change our dynamics somewhat, but at least I wouldn't have to pretend around him.

"What happened? How did they even escape?" I demanded.

Kale erased the slate and quickly wrote another message.

~ Your sister has the ability to free those under telepathic control with a kiss. Once they were able to leave, allies took them to Talaraine. ~

The claim surprised me. Phoenix's power was growing faster than I realized. Rather than risk him reading my emotions, I brushed past him and walked onto the ship and straight to the room I had last time, it was adjacent to a much-needed bathroom and shower.

Our journey was uneventful, and Kale ignored me as much

as I ignored him.

I had hoped my healing ability would fix whatever Megaera did to my ears, but it became apparent with each passing day that my hearing wasn't coming back anytime soon.

CHAPTER 12 – MOTIVATION

On the fourth day, Kale walked into my room without warning. I glared at him but didn't sit up. I had finally found the ideal sleeping position for this horrible mattress, and I wasn't moving from it.

Kale handed me the slate. As usual, he wrote his message before he came to find me.

~ We will be landing on Talaraine soon. ~

"That's nice," I threw the tablet at him, then closed my eyes and pretended to sleep until after I felt the vibration of the door closing behind him.

I didn't get out of the bed until the ship landed and Kale walked into my room. I stood and smirked.

"We are looking for Phoenix and Tai now?"

Kale held out the slate but didn't let me take it.

~ I want to show you what happens to those Megaera chooses not to kill and wants out of the way. This will be your fate if you fail to bring Phoenix back to her, once you've witnessed the deaths of all your loved ones, particularly that daughter you are so fond of. ~

I flinched, but dutifully followed him out of the warehouse where he had hidden the ship. As we walked through the city, not a single person looked at us, a reflection of Kale's skill as a Telepath in subtly convincing everyone to look elsewhere.

He took me to some kind of learning institution, a university most likely, and into an area where there was underground excavation of some ruins.

We walked down into the ruins, then into a large room, and through a concealed panel in the wall. The room we entered was a deep pit, with a spiral walkway down the walls, and the walls were lines with pods filled with people trapped in stasis. He led me around the ramp, driving home the sheer number of pods.

I knew she put people in stasis pods as punishment, but I didn't know that there were so many pods, and on my mother's world!

"Why are you really showing me this?" I asked. He couldn't expect it to stay a secret, not with so many working on digging these ruins out.

He spoke only one word, and I read it easily on his lips.

"Motivation."

Satisfied that I got the message, he led the way back up the ramp, but stopped abruptly when we were on the opposite side from the hidden entrance.

I stepped around him and saw two teens. One of them looked exactly like my brother, only older, with a thick patch over his face. The patch was likely concealing a large scar. The last time I saw Niko, he was a small child, and he had been shot in the face. I assumed the injury had been fatal, but apparently, he had escaped Nexa instead.

Kale moved, and I thought he might have been talking, but his back was to me, so there was no chance of lip reading, and then I saw who he was talking to.

This world had been kind to Phoenix, in the time it took us to get to this planet, she had managed to clear up her skin, cut her hair, and even gain some weight. Tai stood next to her, less gaunt, and with his hair dyed a dark, blood red.

Tai spoke, I was almost positive he called Phoenix 'Nixie.' I turned my attention back to Niko and missed what happened next, barely seeing Phoenix fall down the hole in the center of the room.

I did not miss it when Tai leapt after her. He caught her, then brown feathered wings sprouted from his back, shredding his shirt. His wings effectively slowed his decent, although he couldn't maneuver in the room.

Kale grabbed my arm and held up a stone pendant as smoke covered us. The world shifted, and we were standing in a stone room. Kale shoved me to the ground, said something I had no chance of understanding, and vanished into the same cloud of smoke.

I stood, and realized it was in a room with some kind of power dampener. I could sense my power, but I couldn't access it, not even my telepathy. I spun around. The room was larger than the one I had in the mansion, although it had nothing more than a small wardrobe and a bed.

I walked out of the room, and into a sitting room, with dirty, mismatched couches arranged in a loose triangle. There were two other doors in this room, besides the one that led to the bedroom. I opened the first, and found the bathroom, a tiny room with a weird toilet, and a shower head with a drain in the corner. The second door led to a kitchen, fully stocked with dried food.

I stepped out of the kitchen, back into the sitting room and took a slow, deep breath. There were no other doors in this strange apartment, and no windows at all. Careful searching of the ceiling revealed tiny holes that served as ventilation, but they weren't even big enough to stick my pinky in, let alone search.

I searched the rooms again; this I took my time and was more methodical. The walls were made of polished stone, so were the floors and ceiling. It was possible they were all carved from the same stone, and I could find no seams or imperfections. I could find no way to leave this place, this bunker. There was no way to know if it was in a building, or underground, although I suspected it was buried.

Worst of all, with the power dampener, I couldn't use my magic at all, and magic was required to enter the Betwixt. It was also required to summon Dina with the crystal, something I quickly realized.

CHAPTER 13 -TRIALS OF LEADERSHIP

There was absolutely no way to tell time in the bunker, as I came to think of it. No changes in the lights, or the air flow. That jerk Kale didn't even leave me anything to read. I spent my days hoping this was part of Megaera's plan and that my children were safe. My only distraction when I was awake was to try to remember the dance routines, I taught Phoenix and Kayda when they were little, and to go over my hand-to-hand combat forms over and over until I was too exhausted to continue. When I was hungry, I ate. When I was tired, I slept, and I did a lot of sleeping.

Kale didn't keep me in there forever. Finally, after I stopped keeping track of how often I slept, I woke to find him sitting on one of the nasty couches I had shoved against one wall. He held a bloody knife in one hand.

"Who did you kill?" I demanded, thinking first of Phoenix, then Tai.

He snarled and said something, but he spoke to quickly for me to understand. Once he was done with his rant, he thrust the slate at me.

~You have new orders. You are to enter the Trials of Leadership and be victorious. Your opponent is Phoenix. You are to eliminate her. She has proven without doubt that she will no longer serve as an asset to Nexa. Failure will result in the death of your eldest. I will take you to the cavern where the Trial will take place. You will wait in the cavern until the trials begin. ~

"What is this trial you are talking about?" I asked. I held out the slate.

He snatched it out of my hand and hastily wrote out a message.

~ Defendants of the House of Aphelion, like you through your mother Juliet, enter a cavern and submit to the tests. The unworthy die, and only one is chosen to lead the Duchy of Aphelion. You and Phoenix are the only living descendants of Aphelion eligible. I will sneak into the trial to assist you and ensure your victory. ~

"Wait you locked me in here for who knows how long, and now you want me to enter some trial to rule a duchy?" I held out the tablet. "What else is going on?"

He snatched it from my hand and tossed it on the couch. He stood and grabbed my arm and teleported us out of the room. He shoved me toward a cave opening. I glared back at him but walked into the cave.

Compared to the bunker, the wait wasn't horrible, but I was still thoroughly bored by the time Phoenix walked into the cave, even though I found what I suspected were uncut colalace all over the floor. They had the same sheen as the one that had been on my bracelet.

"I heard your fence post boyfriend call you Nixie. It's cute, and it suits you," I said as I toyed with one of the crystals that cluttered the floor.

Phoenix spoke, and while I wasn't positive, I thought she said something about us not being related. The joke was on her. My birth mother was her birth father's half-brother. We were totally related, but I could mess with her a bit. I was a few years older than her, and her parents would have been teenagers when I was born, but it was possible that they could have had a child my age.

"How sure are you that I'm adopted?" I joked.

The banter was over when two openings appeared in the

cave wall. I slipped the colalace crystal in my pocket and walked to the opening closest to me. It was time to see what these Trials of Leadership entailed.

"See you on the other side," I said.

As soon as I was in the center of the cavern, the opening closed. I was alone in a circular room made of sparkling crystals. I felt the floor vibrate and looked down as loose crystals arranged themselves into words. The words were difficult to make out, the crystals that made them were the same translucent white as the crystal that made up the floor, but I managed.

~ Why have you returned? ~

"Yeah," I drawled. "I've never been here. You must be thinking of someone else."

Apparently, my response was the wrong answer. A crystal shot from the floor toward my face, and I barely managed to block it with the back of my arm. I hissed and glanced at the cut on my arm, it wasn't healing.

The crystals once again rearranged themselves.

~ Why are you here? ~

"It's not like it was my idea," I snapped.

This time, several crystals shot towards me from multiple locations on the floor and wall. I dodged them and used my hands and arms to shield my face. When the barrage ended, I had cuts all over my hands, arms, and a long gash on my foot, as well as a particularly deep one on my ear.

The wall opened, and I quickly walked out of the cave before my sass earned me a few more cuts.

The cave didn't open into another cavern, as I expected. Instead, it opened into a wooded area, with a barrier over the trees, visible by the slight shimmer in the sky. The barrier meant I couldn't flee, and I didn't doubt that Kale was in the woods, to ensure I succeeded.

Rather than risk anyone sneaking up on me, including Kale with his teleportation pendant, I found a tree I could easily climb, even with my damaged hands. Once I was high enough to not be immediately visible, I tried to stop the bleeding by wrapping the worst cuts, but I didn't have enough rags for every cut.

There wasn't time to stress to much about the injuries. Phoenix walked down the path. I jumped out of the tree and realized I couldn't land on my injured foot. Instead of landing steadily, I fell onto my back, then scrambled back to my feet.

"Looks like you survived the questions," I commented as I tried to hold the cut on the back of my hand closed, while keeping my view on her face.

Phoenix didn't speak. Instead, she took her armored jacket off, then her shirt, leaving only a thin undershirt. She used her knife to cut her shirt into strips.

"What are you doing?" I demanded.

Phoenix moved her head when she answered, but I caught the end. She asked why I wasn't healing.

I had figured it out while trying to tend to my wounds in the tree. "Didn't they tell you? We can't heal while the Trials are going on. How else can the crystals take down a dangerous Novem?"

She shook her head as she took my hand and began to wrap it. I let her wrap both arms. This was unexpected kindness. Perhaps she had thrown off the manipulation I had placed on her emotions, although it was impossible to tell. Her mental wall was too strong.

"Aww, you care," I joked as she knelt and wrapped my foot. She started to speak, and I moved to see her face. Having some idea of what she was saying was better than having none at all.

What will it attract? Was she talking about my blood?

"Great, I might attract monsters." I complained. "You know, we wouldn't be in this mess if you had restrained yourself and not kissed a bunch of slaves."

Phoenix scowled, which I expected, then her expression shifted to realization, and excitement.

"Nixie?" I drawled, confused.

As Phoenix climbed to her feet, she spoke, but I had no idea what she said. It was clearly past time to admit I couldn't hear.

She said something, her expression hostile. Something about guards.

"I'm not going to rot in an Aphelion jail," I called as she walked away.

I should have kept my mouth shut. I was pretty sure my words brought Kale to our location.

Phoenix reacted quickly, but Kale brought her to her knees with a telepathic attack. I stumbled towards her. She clutched the grass in her fists as she struggled against whatever command he was forcing into her head.

I needed to distract him! Phoenix was strong enough, she could overpower him, if she had the chance.

"What are you doing here? This wasn't the plan we agreed on. I told you I would take care of this on my own. You need to leave!"

Kale spoke too quickly. I had no chance of understanding him. With a flourish of his hand, Phoenix leapt to her feet, a thick lock of hair fading to white with the motion.

I stared at that white streak of hair, horrified. I thought Phoenix was too strong to fall under the complete control of another telepath.

"Let her go," I snapped at Kale. "You gain nothing from this."

Phoenix flinched away from me, the rage on her face morphed to fear.

"Phoenix?" I said slowly. I found that I couldn't move either, but I wasn't sure if it was a telepathic suggestion or my own reluctance.

Phoenix swung her hands forward, and wind gathered around my head. When she clapped her hands against my ears, the wind slammed into my ears, aggravating the damage Megaera already caused, and bringing back the pain.

I fell to my knees, grabbing my ears the second Phoenix released my head. Blood leaked from my ears, and the world shifted. I threw up at Phoenix's feet, and grabbed the nearby tree, leaning against it until the vertigo subsided enough for me to climb back to my feet.

Phoenix held a knife in one hand, and with her other, she held her arm, as though she were forcing the knife down. Her hair had several more streaks of white. I closed my eyes as the vertigo returned.

When I looked at her again, her arm was raised. She slowly lowered the knife, then relaxed slightly.

I stepped forward, eager to help her escape Kale's control, when the knife flew up again, this time without hesitation.

Fire erupted across my face as the blade slashed through my cheek and up my face through my eye. I fell, the pain and dizziness were too much. There was too much blood pouring down my face, and too much blood had already soaked through the rags.

I looked up with my good eye as Kale and Phoenix fought. Phoenix managed to injure him before he took her knife and pinned her against a tree.

He thrust the knife into her stomach, and she kissed his mouth.

"No!" I screamed as they both fell to the ground.

Kale cradled Phoenix on his knees, horrified by what he had done. The knife was buried to her hilt at an angle in her side. If only she had kept her jacket on, it had looked like armor, it might have been enough to protect her from the blade.

I took the jagged colalace crystal out of my pocket and crawled towards them, but I didn't make it more than a few inches before I fell, too weak. I felt the crystal get snatched out of my hand as the vision in my remaining eye dimmed.

CHAPTER 14- HEALING

Waking was painful. My head hurt, and my face burned. I shifted, relieved that the vertigo was gone, and I realized I was on a bed, covered in a soft blanket. I risked opening my eye. A younger, feminine version of my grandfather stood over me. She held her hands over my ears and the pain in my head faded, replaced by the gentle warmth of her healing magic. She scowled and I read her emotions. She wasn't satisfied with the healing she had just completed. She put her hands back over my ears, but her healing magic only flowed around my ears for a moment before she gave up, and instead put one hand over my injured eye. Her magic chased away the pain, but when I tried to open that eye, nothing in my vision changed.

The woman smiled wanly and stepped away from me. I sat up slowly and looked around. I was in a large room, with windows that let in the dimming light of sunset. The light was a relief, I was sick of being trapped in rooms underground.

The woman took a pad of paper and a glittery pink pen off the counter and wrote on it as she walked back to me. She paused to finish writing, before she handed it to me.

~ I'm sorry, the damage to the bones in your inner ears was too complete to heal. Someone turned them to dust, and I can't fix them. There are hearing aids that can be built for you to replace the function of the inner ear, but it will take time to get them built for you. Your eye is completely gone, but a prosthetic can be made that will restore your vision. Would you object to these enhancements? If there's no objection, I can get the measurements now. ~

I read the message twice and took a slow deep breath. Magic could only heal so much. I knew that, but until now I had hoped.

"I have no objections to these prosthetics," I said hesitantly. "But who are you, and why are you helping me? Come to think of it, where are we, and where are Phoenix and Kale?"

She grinned and took the pad back. She wrote a quick note, then handed it back to me.

~You ask a lot of questions. ~

"I'm a naturally curious person, and even if I wasn't, I think I would still ask those questions." I smiled and handed the pad back and let her write her response.

~ We are family, I think. You entered the Trials of Leadership for Aphelion and survived them. ~

I read the message, then gave the pad back. I was sure we were related, but not on the side of the family that had ties to Talaraine.

"What's your name?" She hadn't answered my questions, so I would simplify my requests.

~ Selena. What's yours? ~

As soon as I read the question, I realized two things. First, Phoenix wasn't in any condition to tell people who I was, and second, she assumed I was an ally. She probably was a friend of Phoenix's, and would possibly arrest me if I revealed myself, but maybe it would also give me a chance to contact Rowan, to check on my kids.

"My name is Hope," I said, careful to stay focused on her emotions.

I had expected hostility, it would confirm my assumption that this woman was a friend of Phoenix's, and surely Phoenix would have warned her friends about her twisted, sadistic sister. Instead, Selena responded with excitement and relief. She wrote furiously.

~ You are in Alpenglow Palace. We found you injured after

the Trials had ended. Duchess Phoenix is alright, and Kale has been arrested. You need to get some rest, but would it be alright if I get measurements for the prosthetics? ~

I bit my lip. She wasn't wrong, I was tired, and it would give me a chance to finally get back into the Betwixt. I wasn't wearing my old clothes, so I didn't have the shard to call Dina, but maybe the Chaos Sprite could be summoned from the Betwixt.

"What do I need to do to for the prosthetic measurements?"

She grinned and wrote another quick message.

~ Just stay still, it's a quick, painless procedure. ~

I nodded and smiled at Selena.

She set the pad down on the small table next to my bed, with the glittery pink pen, and picked up a small clear screen the size of her palm. She held the screen over my left ear, then my right. She checked the information and held it over my ruined eye. When she was done, she reached for the pad, but I took her hand gently in mine.

"I'm really tired," I confessed. Healing magic, especially receiving a healing, was exhausting.

Selena nodded and grinned. She patted my hand, then walked out of the room.

As soon as I was alone, I looked at my arms. The crystals had cut my arms and hands in the same lines as the scars Amara had healed years ago. Perhaps it was a message from the Trials, a reminder that I still had to pay for my past. I curled up under the blanket and found a comfortable position.

The advantage to having my magic blocked for weeks was that I had plenty of reserves, even if I was physically tired. It meant I could enter the Betwixt.

I opened my eyes, relieved to see the familiar garden I had created with Rowan. I sat down under a large tree and waited. I tried calling to Dina, but there was no response. Rowan never showed up, and I would have even settled for Amara, but instead I was awakened before anyone showed up.

Selena took her hand off my shoulder and grinned down at me. She held up the pad, flipped to a new page, with a new message.

~ You need to eat, and you are too dehydrated. I'm going to give you an IV of fluids to help, but you also need to eat something and drink some fluids. ~

"Right," I mumbled. I took my arm out from under the blanket and let her press a needle into my skin and tape it into place. The needle was connected to a tub that led to a canister of clear fluid.

Reluctantly, I sat up, and dutifully ate the brothy soup and drank the sweet juice she offered. She waited, writing a message as I ate. As soon as I was done, she took the try and handed me the pad and a beautiful small box that fit in the palm of my hand. I opened the box and found two small devices, the same shade as my skin. They had soft cone that would fit in my ears, with thin plastic that wrapped around the outside of my ears. I wanted to try them on immediately, but at Selena's prompting, I first read the note.

~ I apologize, I am not as familiar with these prosthetics as I first assumed. You will need to be fully healed, then there is a surgery that will need to be performed. You received a nasty head injury in the trials that hasn't fully healed and will take time. Magic can only heal so much when it comes to such delicate injuries. Once you are healed, we can perform the surgery, then the hearing aids will work. ~

I closed the box and set it on the side table, disappointed.

"Tell me the truth, please. Will this surgery work? Will I be able to hear again?"

Selena hesitated, and I didn't even need my ability to know she wasn't confident.

"What are the chances that I'll be able hear after this surgery?" I asked.

Selena sighed and wrote her response.

~ It depends on how well your injury heals, and what scars remain. I truly believe you will recover enough to use the hearing aids. ~

I handed the pad back and smiled, nervous about what else

I risked learning was no longer what I would get back. "What about my eye?"

~ Tori, a healer you've met, is nearly here with a specialist. The eye will take a bit more work than the hearing aids, but the specialist can start on the exterior as soon as he gets here. He wants to see your good eye in person to ensure both eyes perfectly match. ~

I gasped when I read that and slowly smiled. "Selena, would it be possible to pick the color of my new eye?"

Selena tilted her head in bemusement, then shrugged. She took back the pad, wrote her message, and handed it back to me.

~ It's not a requirement, but wouldn't you rather have matching eyes? I'm told this specialist is so good, it's impossible to tell the prosthetic from the organic eye. ~

"Oh, I'm sure. I've always wanted blue eyes, but I'll settle for one blue eye and one green."

Selena took the pad back, then tensed and turned to the door. She hesitated for a moment, before she walked to the door and opened it. She spoke to whoever was in the hallway, then stepped back and let them into the room.

The new visitors consisted of two men and a stern woman. One of the men was Tori, easy to recognize even though he had gained some weight and cut off most of his hair. The woman pushed to the front of the group and stood right in front of me. The other man began to speak, but he was partially blocked by the woman, who was forming rapid shapes with her fingers as the man spoke.

I stared at her, lost, and turned to Selena. Selena was laughing, the pad and pen uselessly in her hands.

I turned back to the group and looked around the woman. "I can't understand what she is trying to communicate. Are you the specialist, here to make me a new eye? I would like a blue one."

Selena managed to speak through her laughing fit, and whatever she said caused Tori's neck and face to take on a rash-like shade of red. He took the pad from Selena and gave it to the other man, as the stern woman left in a huff.

Like my conversations with Selena, it was a longer process for me to speak, then get the response he wrote down so I could read it. It took even longer for him to explain what he was doing and for us to come to an agreement on what the eye would look like, with him hedging my expectations.

When they finally left, I settled back on my bed, grateful to be alone. I curled up and blinked, but before I fell asleep, the door opened again.

CHAPTER 15 – REVELATION

Whoever opened my door lurked in the hallway, just out of view. I waited, but no one walked in.

"In or out," I called impatiently. "Either way, shut the door." I paused. "And if you're talking, I can't hear you. I'm completely deaf."

Rowan walked in. My breath caught. In the time we had been separated, he had grown a beard, although naturally it was well kept, and he walked into the room with a cane in one hand and a screen in the other.

He paused and I sat up.

"I'm over here," I said.

He walked toward me and found the chair next to my bed. He settled in it, then set his cane on the floor and reached his hand out. I took his hand and clasped it between both of mine.

"Did Selena tell you?" I asked.

He spoke, but I didn't understand him. He wasn't as easy to understand as Phoenix, maybe because she had been yelling at me, or maybe because I grew up with her and knew her so well.

"Rowan...I don't know if you've heard, but I'm deaf. Megaera..." I paused and shook my head, although I knew he couldn't see the motion.

"Yes or no, are the girls safe?"

He nodded and held up the screen. He spoke, and I nearly cried when words rapidly appeared on the screen.

~ They are safe. Crowe and Adalinde have them in a well concealed location. ~

I smiled. Crowe and Adalinde were siblings, and trusted royal guards in Prince Remy's court. They could effectively conceal my children, even from Megaera.

Rowan began to speak again, and more word appeared on the screen.

~What happened? It's been several weeks since I last heard from you, when Dina brought me those strange weapons. ~

I nodded. That was the last time we had any communication, and it was indirect, through Dina.

"There isn't much to the story," I began. I told him my incomplete tale, about the journey to Talaraine that lacked any gravity ribbons to speed our way, and the strange encounter with Niko and Phoenix before I was trapped in the bunker. When I told him of the bizarre trials, he set the screen down and used his hands to carefully check my arms, gently feeling each scar before he checked my face, his fingers barely brushing the socket of my ruined eye.

"It's okay, I'm okay," I said. I bit my lip and picked up the screen, but what could Rowan say? I set it on the nightstand.

When I looked at Rowan, I saw it in the sad set of his smile and felt it in the way he brushed my hair away from my face. He knew I was lying, and he would wait until I was ready to tell the truth.

I felt my lip tremble, and I took a shuttering breath. "I can't hear anything. Megaera destroyed my hearing, and the best I'll get is hearing aids that will just recreate sound, and it will never sound right!" My voice caught and I shook my head. "And that's not the worst part. The worst part is that you have sacrificed more, and you will never get your sight back, and it's all my fault."

Rowan didn't try to find the screen, instead he moved from his chair and sat next to me, wrapping me in a tight embrace. I sobbed, finally safe enough to be afraid, and to grieve.

Once I calmed, Rowan said something, although I didn't have a good enough view of his face to know what he said. He stood and left.

I leaned back, truly exhausted and ready to sleep. I hadn't even stopped crying, not completely.

So naturally I had a second group of visitors. Tori entered first, followed by Phoenix and Tai. I settled into my pillow, tired in every sense of the word, but equally aware that I owed Phoenix whatever information she sought. I wiped my eye and sat up.

They weren't looking at me. In fact, Phoenix and Tai were wrapped up in their own conversation. Phoenix was turned away from me, so I couldn't even try to work out what they were saying. I considered, briefly, being polite or just ignoring them all, before giving up on politeness completely.

"My eye hurts and I suck at lip reading," I said. I picked up the screen and held it out to Phoenix. "Also, I can't interpret the hand movements of that interpreter some idiot healer brought in." I said the last part with a pointed look at Tori. Seriously, when did he think I had time to learn an entirely new language?

Phoenix snatched the screen out of my hand and wrote a quick message. As soon as she was done, she flipped the screen so I could read it while she held it.

~ Did Lord Rowan hurt you? ~

I stared at the message. She had clearly met Rowan, but did she know we were married? Was that fact something Rowan wanted to keep quiet for some reason?

"I'll answer any questions you have about my actions and motivations," I said finally. "But Rowan is personal and none of your business." I snapped my mouth shut. It was probably too much to admit Rowan meant something to me, but the words were said, and I couldn't make her forget them.

Phoenix's eyes narrowed and she rapidly wrote out another message while Tai watched over her shoulder with a smirk.

~ You are not a very good negotiator. I can arrange to have him held here. ~

I stared at the message. Was she threatening me, or was this some clumsy attempt to protect me?

"Really?" I said finally. "He's very influential on Valoria, and therefore he's influential on Karabeeya." I said, naming first the kingdom where we lived, then the planet. "You'll cause an interplanetary incident because of a few tears? Really, use your brain and start acting like the leader that creepy cave thinks you are. Besides, he didn't hurt me. I hurt him. Drop the issue and ask the questions you came for."

Phoenix chewed on her lip and swayed as she considered my rant. After an awkward pause, she typed out her response.

~ Why aren't you using the hearing aids? ~

I stared at her in disbelief. I could well imagine how our interactions had looked from her perspective. I aided the slave master that tormented her and her soulmate, and who knew what chaos Kale caused while I was trapped in that bunker. Yet, she asked about the hearing aids. How did she still care?

"They won't work until I've completely healed, and they do another surgery. That healer, Selena, said they may not work after that. There's brain damage that isn't healing well."

Phoenix was actually fighting back tears as she typed her response. Seriously, where was this compassion coming from?

~ I'm sorry. ~

"Good for you," I snapped.

Tai and Phoenix started talking to each other, again turned just enough that I had no hope of understanding any of what they said.

~ Why did Kale want you dead? ~

I looked down at my hands, at the scar that twisted around my thumb. That was a great question. I wasn't stupid, the trials were possibly the best chance he had of finding Phoenix alone, and my prolonged stay in the bunker implied they weren't dumb enough to trust me, and that could have even been after the girls were safe and they had nothing else to threaten me with.

My biggest fear was that there was something I was missing, some piece I didn't know about and therefore couldn't understand the full picture. Was that why Rowan hadn't told them about us? Or had he been waiting for me to make the choice.

With a sigh, I nodded to myself. "I guess I'll tell you everything," I said.

CHAPTER 16 – AGREEMENT

Phoenix kicked the bed and I looked up to see the screen shoved in my face.

~Don't lie, and don't stop me from finding out if you are lying. ~

I brushed my hair out of my face and thinned my mental wall. "I'm too tired to block out empaths," I tried to make it sound like a joke, although it probably came out as the awkward truth it was.

"After you were… sold…" I cringed inwardly at the word, but when Phoenix didn't respond, I pressed on. "Megaera would send me to check on you every couple of weeks, with a few guards. After the third time I was sent to check on you, our dad helped me escape… I lived on Karabeeya for a while, although Dad meant for me to go to Talaraine. Then, I made a mistake and Megaera found me. That was not a pleasant experience, but I managed to convince her I was a prisoner on Karabeeya, not a runaway. I was to prove my loyalty by finding you and bringing you back. Instead, I contacted Kahlan and told him how to find Yue Equinox, which led them to you. I stayed with Kale and tried to frustrate his plans. Kale caught on and when Setne arranged for the old Duke's death, I went into the Trials as ordered and deliberately tried to fail. That cavern didn't view me as a threat to Aphelion, which is what I expected, but it didn't really like me either."

~ You tried to die? ~

I shrugged, I didn't really think of it like that, but what choice did I have? "As opposed to what? Jumping every time Setne snapped his fingers? What life is that? If I died, he couldn't use me anymore." If I had died, what would have happened to my daughters? It wasn't a terrifying thought, tempered only by the memory of Rowan's assurance that they were fine.

Phoenix frowned at my admission, then typed her response.

~ Are you loyal to Setne? Will you help him if he contacts you? ~

I shook my head. Setne wasn't the real threat, I was almost positive he was more like Tai, close to breaking but ultimately, he could heal from his experience. Still, even though he was just a puppet, he was the face of everything Phoenix feared.

"I'll try not to," I said honestly. I was too tired, and unbidden, the thought of Athena one day experiencing what it was like to lose one sense and have another hindered hit me and tears streamed down my face. I would do it again, I realized. I would hurt my sister to protect Athena from this fate.

Phoenix kicked the bed again and held out the screen.

~ I can help you block whoever controls you. ~

I shook my head. Explaining what I really feared meant revealing my children, and I wasn't sure what measures were keeping them safe. A glance at my sister, with the streaks of white in her hair, solidified my resolve. Phoenix could be Megaera's next unwilling puppet, her wall had broken once, it would break again.

~ Trust me, Hope. Trust me when I say you will be safe here, and we can help you. Stay here with us. ~

I closed my eye and leaned back against the headboard. It was my fault. I created the situation that cause so much pain. I hurt her, yes to protect others in my family, but it didn't make my choices forgivable. I would stay, at least long enough to ensure she was safe from further actions by Megaera.

"I don't trust anyone here. Not anymore, but... I'll stick around." I couldn't resist a small smile. "I'll even do my best to behave."

I expected they would either take the hint and let me sleep, or Phoenix would kick the bed again to get my attention. I didn't expect Phoenix to sit on the bed next to me and wrap one arm around my shoulders. I rested my head against her shoulder and took a long, deep breath.

"Thank you," I said as she rested her head against mine. I relaxed, and after a few minutes she pulled away and typed out another message.

~ We'll let you get some sleep. ~

"Thank you," I sighed. I watched them leave before I finally relaxed enough to fall asleep.

CHAPTER 17 -THE FAMILY GROWS

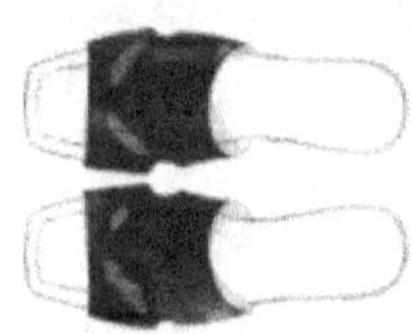

I thought I would spend several days in bed, but the healer Selena's skills were better than I realized, and I woke with a headache, and enough energy to get out of bed and take a shower. The heat from the shower did wonders, and the clothes left out for me were comfortable and baggy, with long sleeves that covered most of my hands and plush sandals that were like walking on a mattress.

Reluctant to get back in the bed, I sat in the chair next to the bed and toyed with the screen. With it, I had access to the public information of Talaraine, including the musings of their snips, public commentors that shared information and opinion interchangeably.

It wasn't their opinions I was interested in, merely the images of the royal family. When I saw the image of the two sisters, I laughed out loud. Selena, my healer, was the crown princess. Perhaps my sister was naturally so compassionate, but I couldn't help but wonder if she was motivated less by altruism, and more by curiosity. Did she know we were related? Did she suspect we were sisters? Did I want her to know?

The lights flickered and I glanced at the door. It had been an update while I slept. The lights would flicker when someone came to my door, giving me the option to allow them entry or ignore them, and trust my wishes would be respected.

"You may enter," I called.

The door opened, revealing a tall man with pure white hair pulled back in a loose, messy ponytail at the name of his neck. At first glance, I thought it was Kale, but no. This man was older, and there was little resemblance beyond the height and hair. His eyes were green, and he held a small screen in his hands. We had the same green eyes, the same stubborn chin.

I recognized him, although it was difficult to reconcile his presence with the information. I had been looking up images of my family, debating if I wanted to reach out to them, if I wanted them to know the daughter, they believed dead was alive, albeit one who would not meet their expectations.

After the briefest hesitation, he slowly held up the screen so I could read it.

~ May I come in? ~

"Sure," I said. Belatedly, I thinned my mental walls to read his emotions. He was nervous, but there was nothing to indicate another telepath controlled him, and there was nothing to indicated he was repulsed by me.

He stepped into the room, then glanced uncertainly from me to the door. He cringed, then glanced back at me and mimed closing the door, then leaving it open.

I smiled faintly at his willingness to communicate with me, no matter how awkward the attempts.

"You can close the door," I said. "Take a seat."

He glanced around. He had two choices, a stool in the corner, or the bed. He took the stool from the corner and moved it, so it was in front of me, across the room.

He smiled. He couldn't seem to conceal his nervousness, a trait I would have expected the consort of a world leader to have mastered after over two decades.

He swiped on his screen then turned it back to me.

~My name is Etan Paxa. ~

I smiled and set my own screen on the nightstand, face down.

"I know who you are." I paused, then decided to test him. "My uncle, Blaze, told me about you."

Etan tensed and looked down at his screen, then looked back at me without writing anything, lost.

I nodded once and took a deep breath. I was tempted to raise every defense, but I had to know the truth, which meant facing it directly. "He said you were my father."

Etan nodded and typed out a quick response.

~ A DNA test confirmed it. ~

The message was turned to me for only an instant, barely enough time for me to read it before he tensed and scowled, although it looked like he was more upset with himself than me. He flipped the screen back to him and typed out a different message.

~ I'm glad you are here. ~

"Despite the circumstances that brought me here?"

He typed furiously, and I resolved to find a more efficient method of communication.

~We interrogated Raiden, the man you knew as Kale. He told us you were being blackmailed into compliance, and when those his master threatened were safe, his orders changed. He said the goal was for Phoenix to kill you, and he was to use the resulting trauma to subdue her and take her to Nexa. ~

"Phoenix managed to free him?" I asked.

Etan nodded.

~ It's not impossible. ~

I looked pointedly at his own pure white hair. He was like Kale, he had given up his free will to be the slave of another, and someone saved him. It was a story I hoped to hear one day, but now was not the time to ask.

"Etan, can Kale, or you, be controlled by another telepath?" I had heard that once someone like Tai broke free, they couldn't be controlled again, but did that apply to those who had fallen completely under another influence?

Etan shook his head and typed out another message.

~ There have been extensive tests, telepaths like Megaera can't influence me. ~

I nodded once. There was truth in his words, and a confidence that came from external confirmation rather than self-assurance.

"Megaera was threatening my daughters. They are in hiding, but my husband is here. Rowan Argentia. He's a good man, very kind, but I haven't told Phoenix about him, or my girls yet." I held up the hearing aids. "I was hoping to stay long enough to get the surgery for these to work. Selena said I had to finish healing first. The only reason I would leave sooner would be for my girls. They are safely in hiding and are safer without me. That could change."

Etan smiled sympathetically.

~ Would you like a tour of the gardens? I would love to hear more about your children. ~

I laughed. "Getting out of this room sounds great."

CHAPTER 18 – COMMUNICATION

After the tour, Etan offered to take me to Rowan's room. He left me in front of the door, and I appreciated that he wasn't trying to force a relationship neither of us was ready for.

I knocked on the door, then realized if he gave a verbal response, I'd have no way of knowing.

"It's me!" I shouted.

The door opened, revealing a teenage girl. I stepped back. Had Etan brought me to the wrong room? The girl looked familiar, and it only took a moment to place her as the girl from the ruins who was with Niko, Phoenix, and Tai.

Before I could offer an apology and ask for directions to the right room, Rowan stepped into view. His beard was gone, giving me a clear view of his mouth as he spoke my name.

I grinned and stepped past the teen to take Rowan's hand. He clasped my hand in both of his, then wrapped me in a tight embrace.

When he released me, and I stepped back with reluctance, I saw Niko had joined his friend.

I smiled nervously at my brother. He had been a small child the last time I saw him.

Rowan motioned to the couches, and we all sat down, Rowan on one side of me, and Niko's enthusiastic friend on the other.

I watched as she typed out a message on a small screen.

~Hello Hope! My name is Rikki, and I'm a friend of Niko's. We are going to teach you and Rowan sign language so the two of you can more easily communicate if your surgery doesn't work. ~

"How are you going to teach Rowan sign language?" I asked hesitantly.

Rikki held up one finger and grinned before she moved to where Rowan sat. She took his hands and clasped them around hers. She brought one hand to her chest, fingers spread out, then brought her hand out. It was difficult to see what she was doing, with Rowan's hands over hers. Then she released his hand. He brought his hand to his chest then pulled it away from his chest and touched his thumb to his middle finger before flicking his fingers in a smooth motion. He brought his hand up in a fist with the pinky and thumb extended.

Rikki took the screen and typed out a quick message. ~Like this. ~

Rikki pointed to the message and repeated the movements Rowan did.

I followed her example.

"Doing this literally means 'Like this'?"

Rikki nodded enthusiastically.

Rowan turned and had a quick conversation with Niko, who walked into the room and shyly took the screen from Rikki.

~I'm happy to see you Hope. ~

I grinned at Niko. "How did you get here, Niko?"

It took a while to get the story from Niko, and even longer for him type it out, but it was quite the story.

When Niko was young, the Nexan compound where we lived was attacked, and in front of me and Phoenix, someone shot him in the head. The bullet went through his eye and out the side of his head, and his mother, Mirage, used a teleportation crystal to send him to Alpenglow, the city we were in.

Niko was lucky, he was found by a healer who saved his life, then adopted him at the request

Niko was lucky, he was found by a healer who saved his life, then adopted him at the request of the previous Duke. He grew up, safe and happy, getting into trouble with his best friend Rikki, although I suspected she was the troublemaker, and he was the unwilling Tag-a-long. I was relieved to hear of his life, including some stories about his adopted father, the trouble he and Rikki managed to get into, and his current interests in technology and reverse engineering tech that has been found on far off worlds and brought to Talaraine for study.

It was late when Niko and Rikki left. I would have happily spent the night learning of their adventures, but they both had parents who were only willing to put up with missing children for so long.

EPISODE 19 – TELEPATHY

"This seems like an awful lot of trouble. The surgery will be in a few days, and if we're already learning an entire new language, it's like we've already given up."

I buried my face in the crook of his neck. As the tears hit his neck, Rowan flinched then tightened his embrace. I felt his power brush against my mental wall. I thinned my wall and opened my mind to telepathic communication. It meant he could feel all of my fear that the surgery wouldn't work, and he knew what I did to Phoenix, but he took it all in without judgement or condemnation.

We can still communicate like this, he assured me as he tightened his embrace and I moved so I was sitting in his lap. I relaxed against him and hastily pulled away to wipe my face on the back of my sleeve.

The girls will be here in a couple of days, but I have not told our hosts of their existence.

A quick snoop through his memories revealed he didn't even tell them about our marriage. I grinned and rested the side of my face against his so he could feel the smile. I saw other memories too; of the time I was away and his struggle to find the traitor and protect our daughters. I saw too, his struggle with his vision loss, the feelings he wanted to keep from me and accepted that he couldn't.

It was a twisted sort of comfort, to know that he wanted as badly as I did to be able to interact with the world as confidently as before his injury.

I kissed his cheek and his embrace tightened, pulling me even closer against him. This was another way we could communicate, without sight, without sound.

The next morning, Rowan led me to another room where we waited until Etan, Queen Juliet, and a young teen about the same age as Athena walked into the room.

I studied Queen Juliet, recognizing so many of her features as my own. Her hair was caramel brown and lacked the white streaks in my hair. We shared the same skin tone, the same build, the same stubborn chin and thick lips. Only our eyes were different. I had Etan's green eyes, and her eyes were the color of melted amber.

"You must be Queen Juliet," I said. I stood and gave a smooth curtsy, careful not to duck my head, which would have been considered an insult on Talaraine.

Juliet spoke, and I didn't bother to try and read her lips. Rowan and I had settled on a more effective method of communication, at least between the two of us.

She says she doesn't want you to bow to her. You are her daughter.

I leaned against Rowan as he wrapped one arm around me. I let him speak for me. I had been ready to meet Etan, but not the Queen who learned of her cowardly Nexan daughter.

The teen approached me and handed me a small screen.

~Hello. I'm Dani. We're sisters. You look so much like Mom. You could be her clone. I can't wait to see how you look all dressed up in court regalia. ~

I smiled up at Dani then snapped my gaze back to the screen.

Clone.

"I forgot. Megaera sent a clone and a slave to Talaraine. They might be the backup plan. Rowan..." I looked at him as he grabbed his screen and began to talk to it.

Quickly, as he presumably called our children's caretaker, I pulled Etan to the side. I wasn't sure if I was talking loudly or quietly and didn't want to risk talking over him.

"Megaera has clones of herself, all telepaths. She sent one to Talaraine with a slave, possibly another telepath, like Kale."

Etan nodded and took out his screen.

~Do you know where they are? ~

I shook my head. "I doubt I was supposed to know of the clone. Setne told me."

Etan raised an eyebrow and I rushed to explain my theory.

"Setne sometimes acts differently, like he's two people. Growing up, I always thought it was his madness, signs of a fractured insanity. But lately... But lately I've been wondering if he's a slave like Kale, only he can resist the telepath who controls him."

Etan listened, and he was receptive to my theory, I could sense it in his emotions, I could also sense the moment my words resonated with some memory or knowledge of his own that confirmed my theory for him.

He turned and spoke to Juliet, and I took a step back to impatiently wait for them to finish.

Instead, with smiles and waves, they left.

"What just happened?" I asked.

You gave them much to think about, and the threat of a Megaera clone is not something that can be dismissed. Etan will ensure people are on guard against such a threat.

I sighed and took Rowan's hand in mine.

Hope, we don't have to stay here. We can leave tomorrow after the surgery for your eye. I'm sure we can find another healer for your hearing. We can stay with the girls, away from whatever machinations this clone is enacting.

I squeezed his hand. He wasn't wrong, and it looked like Etan had the resources to handle the threat. I could come back when it was safe, to introduce my daughters to my new family, and I had been away from the girls for far too long.

I agree. Let's leave tomorrow evening. I'm sure Phoenix will be relieved to get rid of me.

I winced as I realized he could sense my emotions and knew how much it hurt to have lost Phoenix's support as a sibling.

CHAPTER 20- HOSTAGES

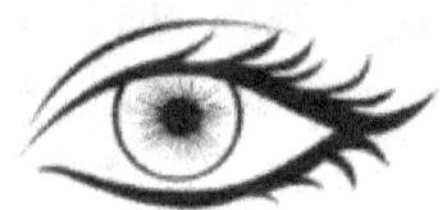

The surgery was a simple one. A tiny chip implanted to help my brain interpret the signals from my new eye. At the same time, the chip for my hearing was implanted, although I wasn't quite healed enough for the hearing aids.

My prosthetic eye took a little… adjusting to.

It didn't just relay images. With a focused thought I could zoom in on something or get an accurate measurement. There was even a program that followed the motions of someone's mouth and gave me text of what was said.

I insisted on trying that new program with anyone willing to endure my curiosity, which meant I spent a lot of time with Rowan (because of course my husband would put up with it) and Dani and Rikki (due mostly to their talkative natures) getting the hang of the program. Despite my normal ability to heal quickly, whatever damage Phoenix did wasn't healing right.

Right before we prepared to leave Talaraine, Rowan abruptly walked to the door and opened it to reveal Phoenix waiting in the doorway.

"You really were going to leave without a word to me?" Judging from the way she maintained careful eye contact and spoke slowly and carefully; she was aware of the program in my new eye.

"Thank you for your generous hospitality," I said with a

smile. Etan had the resources to protect her, there wasn't anything I needed to do that others couldn't do better.

Phoenix's gaze flickered to Rowan with a slight scowl.

I shifted. I hadn't told her the truth, but we hadn't made any effort to conceal our relationship either.

Phoenix bit her lip, then twisted and grabbed her screen out of her pocket. She stared at the screen with naked horror then glared at me. She curled her lip, a warning that she was about to say something cutting, then changed her mind and moved to stand next to me. She thrust the screen in my face and played the short video she had just watched.

It was the Megaera clone, standing in a small room, with Kayda by her side. I stared at my cousin. The last time I had seen her was the day I had walked into her classroom and cut off her ear at the bidding of Megaera. She had been fourteen then. Now she was an adult. She still had the same Cherubic features. Her hair was odd, she had dyed the top half blonde, leaving the bottom half her natural burnt auburn, and had it curled and braided so it swept over her shoulder and completely concealed her missing ear.

The Megaera clone spoke quickly, and kept turning to Kayda, so my program was only catching some of the words.

Hope, the woman in that recording is announcing that her companion will personally kill every member of the Talaraine royal family and the Grand Duchess of Aphelion. Rowan managed to restrain his horror as he relayed the message through our bond. I had no doubt it was an attempt to keep me calm, but calm was impossible.

Sweet Kayda, the kindest of all of us, was a soon to be assassin.

Rowan, the slave is Kayda. The clone wants to use Kayda to kill my family. I couldn't mask me fear, I wasn't as good at modulating my emotions as Rowan, so my statement was laced with my fear and horror. I couldn't walk away from this., I couldn't let them twist Kayda. the way they twisted me.

"How old is this message?" I asked Phoenix.

"There's more," Phoenix retorted.

I watched the video, unsure as to why, I couldn't see what they were saying, then the video panned and showed a cage containing Niko and Rikki. Kayda walked to the cage and pointed at Rikki, who collapsed to the ground.

Rowan, it's Niko and Rikki. Kayda has them. It should have been impossible, we had just had lunch with the two, only a few short hours ago!

I heard.

Phoenix waved to get my attention. "Queen Juliet has restricted interplanetary travel, but it's nearly impossible to stop teleportation. I don't know how long they will stay here."

"They're in the university ruins, I recognize that room," I said.

"I know. Stay here, I can't risk you causing any disruptions." She glanced at Rowan. "Either of you."

She shut the door on her way out and I tried the door, but of course it was locked.

"She locked us in here," I said indignantly. "Why show the video if she didn't want my help?"

Does she know what kind of help you can offer her?

"I doubt it, since she seems to have forgotten I have a way with locks." I pressed my hand against the door near the locking mechanism Just a thread of my power, a tendril that wrapped the locking mechanism and charged with kinetic energy. It wasn't enough to cause an explosion, just enough to force the lock to disengage. I opened the door and checked the hallway. Phoenix apparently had so much faith in the lock that she felt guards were an unnecessary redundancy.

"Security's a bit lax," I commented as I led Rowan out of the hallway.

We'll need to get out of the building to bypass the internal security. Rowan's words were accompanied by the memory of a guard explaining the security systems to Rowan. With it was also a memory of Phoenix needing to be rescued after climbing the side of the palace, and a nearby receiving room with a large balcony.

"How is it that I'm the reckless one?" I asked airily. We ran down the hallway, to the receiving room and out onto the balcony.

Rowan tossed his cane over the side of the balcony, then climbed over the side with far more confidence than I would have managed without my sight. I climbed after Rowan, and he managed to reach the ground before me. He searched furtively for his cane. I grabbed it and thrust it into his hand, then looked around.

"What now?" I asked.

Rowan shrugged and walked slowly until he found the path, then he followed it with more confidence. I trotted to catch up and walked by his side and out of the way of his cane.

Can you drive us to the ruins?

I nodded, then stiffened and gave a verbal affirmation, hoping there were signs that would direct me to the university.

Rowan led the way to an underground garage filled with different hover vehicles. Rowan searched the wall until he found a panel and he tapped it.

The keys are in here, can you open this panel?

"You insult me by asking," I said as I pressed my hand against the panel. This time I used just a little too much power and the panel fell off its hinges. I grabbed a fob and held it up, when nothing happened, I dropped it and grabbed another, then another. The fourth fob reacted to a nearby hovercar, an egg-shaped thing with no windows. I led Rowan to the vehicle and climbed in when the door slid open. Inside, there were no clear controls, and I shared an image of the interior with Rowan.

Working together, we figured out the holo-screen that control the hover vehicle, and I found the ruins in the database. The vehicle lifted off the ground and shot smoothly forward, although it was a little disconcerting to know we had no control over the journey, other than imputing the destination.

It was a tense journey. It occurred to me that where this thing was so automated, it was possible Phoenix could shut it down or redirect the hover vehicle without me knowing any different. When I shared my fear with Rowan, he impatiently retorted that Phoenix was likely just as worried about the two teens as I was, and wouldn't waste her time personally chasing after me, she would have someone else do it.

It wasn't comforting to know a stranger might try to stop us, I wouldn't know how well they would fare against me and I might hurt them more than Phoenix would forgive, or worse.

When the vehicle finally stopped, I carefully climbed out, but saw no waiting ambush, even better, we were near the ruins, but not so close to draw the ire of the guards. It seemed I wasn't the only one who recognized the room.

I grabbed Rowan's arm and tried to warn him of obstacles as I led him to the concealed tunnel I used with Kale.

The tunnel led directly to the room. I made Rowan open the door so he could make sure we didn't make noise. Unfortunately, we were too far from Kayda and the clone for Rowan to hear them and the light was too dim for me to understand them even if I could risk being in their line of sight.

I risked a look around the higher levels of the room, with my eye's enhancements, I saw a heat smudge, that probably belonged to a couple of people, at least.

Can you sense that?

Sense what? I scowled at Rowan. I couldn't risk using my telepathy in the same area as two hostile telepaths! And he shouldn't risk it either!

The clone is forcing her will on Kayda. She wants her to kill Niko and Rikki.

Well, I wasn't about to allow that.

CHAPTER 21 – DRAGON WINGS

I sprinted toward them and sensed *something* in the shadows above me. It was a tangible energy my own power easily connected to. Drawing on that energy, I felt charged. The fatigue of healing from the morning's mild surgeries vanished, and power raced through my veins. As I ran my face and hands began to itch, my hair loosened from the ponytail, and a burst of pain on my back was the instant warning before something ripped my shirt off, leaving my in the camisole I wore under the baggy monstrosity.

I jumped and *floated* on something pulling on my back.

The clone whipped around and saw me, her eyes wide with fear and rage. She snatched Kayda's wrist and they vanish the instant before I caught them.

I landed on my feet, and looked around, to see if they were still in the room.

And I was immediately distracted by the huge wings attached to my back. The feathers were rich browns, caramel and gold, and the wingspan was easily twelve feet.

I felt something, like when someone strokes my hair but instead the sensation came from a wing on my back, it was odd, to suddenly have two more limbs. I shifted, to see what caused the strange new sensation, and found Rowan stroking a wing and talking to the shadows.

I moved to better see who he was talking to.

Phoenix walked out of the shadows, followed by her freakishly tall admirer. He stared at my wings, then my face.

I ran my tongue over my teeth, feeling the elongated canines and sharply serrated molars. If I bit my tongue with these teeth, I risked biting it clean in half with minimal effort.

Noticing that the tree was still staring at my head, I ran my fingers, with freakishly long nails, over my face. My eyebrows were fluffy, and my ears were tapered into long points. My hair was longer, and there were feathers in my hair. I plucked one and it stung as badly as ripping the remnants of a broken nail off.

I winced, and the tree winced in sympathy as blood trickled down my forehead.

Phoenix shook her head at my stupidity and went to help her other companions get Niko and Rikki out of the cage, leaving us with the tree.

"Tai, it's rude to stare," when he continued to stare at me. When he didn't respond I toyed with the feather I plucked out of my head. It was surprisingly soft, and the color was caramel with gold highlights that caught the dim light with a glimmer.

When I looked up at Tai, he was still staring.

"Can I help you?"

"I had no idea you were a dragon," he finally said.

"I'm not, I'm a Novem," I glanced at Rowan. I had only seen two Dragons take a form other than their human one, and neither of them had *feathers.*

Although, admittedly, the secondary forms they had taken were vastly different.

My face has changed. I informed Rowan. *Could that be a dragon thing?*

Rowan nodded slightly and made his way around my awkwardly huge wings. When he stood in front of me, he ran his hands gently over mine, then up my arms to my face where his gentle touch lingered over my bizarre ears, misshapen mouth, and the feathers growing out of my head.

You are a descendant of Talaraine Dragon Royalty.

My mother has dragon blood?

Extremely unlikely given Talaraine's political history. Your father might, he has a more diverse background.

How do you know?

I researched your family history. You father's father comes from a long line of Novem, but your father's mother is a Desmian, and the Desmians often intermingled with Dragons. It's possible at some point she had an ancestor from the royal line.

Great, I'm part Novem, part Desmian, and part Dragon?

It explains your power, although usually the first time a Dragon takes second form it's under extreme emotional distress, and it happens when they are a toddler, not an adult.

I considered that. *Maybe it's because I'm only part dragon? That clone was threatening my family. I think that qualifies as emotional duress.*

Rowan didn't respond, and I was tired of watching Tai stare at me.

"Hey, how do I change back?" I asked. I figured since Tai and Rowan were both dragons, one of them could tell me how to go back to normal.

Rowan placed his hands on either side of my face and leaned his forehead against mine.

Focus on your breathing. Take a deep breath in, slowly. Now, slower still exhale. Do it again…And again. Now, let your shoulders relax as you breath.

I followed his instructions and felt the weight on my back vanish in an instant, as my jaw shifted, and I could feel the feathers pop painlessly out of my skin. When I opened my eyes, I was back to normal, the ground littered with feathers.

Rowan took his hands off my face, and I slid into his arms, burying my face into his neck. I felt weak and may not have been able to stand on my own, but more than that, I was afraid.

Phoenix just told us that the tracker her friend Shay managed to hit Kayda with is showing they are teleporting to several places in quick succession. It's a technique to make it difficult to follow them. She says we should all head back to recover, especially Niko and Rikki.

Are they hurt?

Only mild injuries. Niko is standing behind you. He wants to know if you are okay.

I pulled away from Rowan and maneuvered my face into a calm smile before I turned around. Niko looked filthy, and pale, but unhurt.

"Are you alright?" I asked. I reached out to him, then let my arms fall to my side, as much as I longed to hug my little brother, I didn't want to hurt him.

He nodded and glanced back at the two people fussing over Rikki. I wasn't sure but given that the man was as tall and slender as Rikki, with the same narrowed eyes, silky black hair, and high cheekbones, I guessed they were her parents, or at least the man was a close relative.

"What about you, Hope? Are you alright?"

"I have a mystery to solve, but I'll solve it soon enough. I'm not sure where the dragon blood came from." I meant the statement as a joke, but Niko nodded slowly and adjusted his eye patch.

"You will have to do a DNA test. If either the Queen or her consort had Dragon blood, they would have used that to encourage better treatment of the dragons on Talaraine, it wouldn't be a secret."

I glanced at Rowan. I thought his explanation the most likely, but perhaps a DNA test would confirm it, or clarify my origins. Etan had done one to establish paternity, so they likely weren't difficult to get on this world.

CHAPTER 22 – DRAGON BLOOD

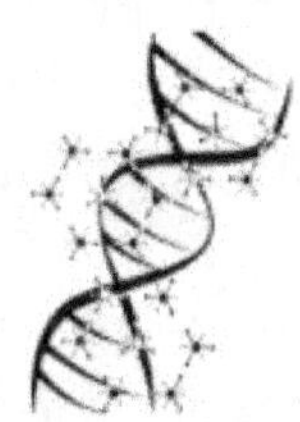

I had to lean on Rowan the entire way back to our hovercraft, and Phoenix insisted on riding with us, convinced I was incapable of keying in the right coordinates. I didn't remember that trip, beyond her climbing in after us, nor did I remember how I reached Rowan's room, but I must have, because I woke in his bed, sprawled over his chest.

I shifted, my cheek damp, and realized I had drooled in my sleep.

"Ew," I groaned.

Rowan jerked with a suppressed chuckle.

"Sorry," I mumbled. I rolled onto my side of the bed and wiped my face with my sleeve.

Rowan shifted and patted my shoulder comfortingly.

I called Tatsu. I told him we would be a few more days. He wondered about bringing the girls here. It might not be a bad plan.

"The plan was to return to Karabeeya and lay low for a while. Let the royalty of Talaraine deal with this mess. They're better equipped," I argued.

Is that still what you want? Even knowing Kayda is one of Megaera's victims?

I sighed heavily and curled up against him. "No." I mumbled. I wanted to protect my children, but I also had to help Kayda. Even if Phoenix was better able to help Kayda, I owed it to her to help with the effort.

I think the children will be safe here. Especially with Tatsu protecting them. It will give you time to help your sister, and time to learn more of how you came to possess dragon blood. Phoenix has asked one of her scientists to look closer at the DNA sample that was used to establish paternity.

I took a long, slow breath. Phoenix would be angry when I revealed my children to her, but it was the last of my secrets, and I could help with the search and eventual rescue of Kayda with my family close.

"Are we overstaying our welcome?"

Doubtful, I think your parents are eager to get to know you.

I nodded and the motion was felt by Rowan.

I would have stayed with him for the entire day, but curiosity compelled me to respond when the scientist contacted Rowan. I went to meet her alone, so Rowan could make arrangements with Etan.

I followed Rowan's directions to the lab. It was in the basement of a large, pristine pink building, monitored by alert but friendly guards. I had the impression that if I did not have an invitation, nothing would have gotten me into the building.

The lab was a large room with a labyrinth of equipment. I stepped around a table with several humming metal containers and saw two pods, identical to the ones in the ruins. The only difference was these were horizontal, not vertical. I walked to the pods, curious. These weren't as filthy as the pods in the ruins, although they showed signs of being recently cleaned, and the metal and glass was too scratched to be able to see into the pod.

Still, I sensed something in the pod on the left. I thinned my mental wall. I couldn't get more than a vague impression before my concentration was ruined by the approach of another, a shadow that merged with mine.

"Who is she?" I asked, then turned so I could get the answer.

Shayla. I recognized her as Rikki's mother. Which meant she was my aunt, Etan's sister. I smiled as I saw the resemblance between her and her twin brother.

"I'm impressed you could tell the pod contains a female," Shayla said. "We don't know who she is. I'm having a hard time bypassing the code to open the pod correctly. If it's opened improperly, she'll die. This is one of the newer pods, there are some that are centuries old."

"We don't know who she is, other than a powerful telepath. I'm having trouble getting the code on the pod to open it. If it's opened improperly, she'll die. I do know this is one of the newer pods, some are centuries old."

"So how old is this one?" I asked.

Shayla exhaled and examined the pod. "Between fifty and seventy years old."

"It's one from the ruins?"

"Yes, we think it's the last one that was stored there, then they were left alone until Kale took you to the room. Apparently, these are enemies Megaera wanted out of the way without killing."

"Even the old ones?" I asked.

"An enchantress can extend her life by killing her heirs, and she has been doing it for at least three Millenia, although it's only been the last fifty years that she's been an active tyrant."

"What changed?" I asked. Three thousand years was an awfully long time to be idle if taking over the Amaranth Empire was her goal.

Shayla shrugged. "I'm not a historian, I only consulted with one on the mystery of these pods. The one behind you is the newest pod, this one here is the oldest." She walked around another table and showed me a rock encrusted pod with glass so scratched it looked white.

She tapped my shoulder to get my attention. "What can you tell me about that occupant?"

I turned back to the pod and thinned my mental wall. There was no aura, and no instinctive knowledge of the occupant, but as I focused on the mystery person, I was able to learn something.

"Whoever they are, they are in the Betwixt."

I sensed Shayla's confusion. Her emotions were easy to read.

"The Dream Realm. It's said that telepaths created it as a refuge, and a prison. I think whoever this is, had a hand in expanding parts of the Dream Realm, I recognize the magic of the Overgrown Gardens. Their mind is deep in the Dream Realm, I won't be able to find them without knowing more about them."

Shayla shook her head. "Male, and not of any species I know."

I sighed. "It's another mystery. You said they are victims of Megaera?"

Shayla nodded. "Speaking of mysteries. You didn't come here for the pods. Come with me."

She led me to another part of the lab, where a small round table with three chairs was set up in the corner. She sat first, and I sat across from her. I only had to wait a few seconds before she spoke.

"Have you heard of the Royal House of D'Valoria?" Shayla asked.

I scowled. Of course, I knew the Royal House of D'Valoria. My husband and I were part of their court, and our daughter was recently chosen to be the Royal Companion to the daughter of the Crown Prince and his wife.

"I've heard of them," I deadpanned.

"There is a story. The dragon king of ancient times had two sons, equally worthy to rule, and to determine who would rule all dragons, each was given a world, and a people to lead. The better leader would become the ruler over all people, and his brother's descendants would submit to his for all time. The older brother ruled Karabeeya, but he valued loyalty above all else, and did not maintain control of the entire planet, instead creating many states that maintained their own governments, and there was peace, but the king questioned the wisdom of his son freely giving away power. The younger son ruled the entire planet, valuing unity. The dragon king was pleased and passed on his title to the younger son."

I held in a sigh, this sounded like a myth to me.

"In time, it was nearly forgotten that D'Valoria was the House of the older son, until the Novem came. The Warrior sought control of the dragons and went to the world with the single government. He tricked the Dragon King, married his daughter, then killed all royal dragons, except the bride that escaped him, to curse the dragons of the world and enable the children of his beloved to rule the planet in place of the dragons. The dragons of Talaraine would have been eliminated entirely, but the Warrior was killed, and the Dragons alone knew where his sole heir was, so they were allowed to live, but D'Valoria did not get involved in the situation, even when the Novem changed the name of the world to Talaraine, and changed the magic of the world to better suit Novem magic."

"You make our ancestors sound like the villains in that story," I joked. It wasn't a complete surprise, I had heard stories before that cast the Novem in a negative light, especially after leaving Nexa.

Shayla tapped the table. "It's more than a story, it's history, and it's important. Ryo didn't tell me the full story until I got the results from your DNA test, then mine. The Dragons don't want outsiders to know D'Valoria is Dragon royalty descended from the original Dragon King." She scowled slightly and shook her head slightly, clearing away the resentment that came with that statement.

"Dragons from that specific line take a final form of a feathered dragon that rules the skies. The dragon blood came from your great grandmother. She was a courtesan in the Amaranth Empire, the mother of Danton Paxa, my father, and your grandfather. I will study this further, but I can tell you that I don't have dragon magic. You, on the other hand, can use Dragon magic as easily as Novem or Desmian magic."

I stared at her. "Why me?" I demanded.

Shayla sighed. "If I knew that, I would tell you. It shouldn't be possible for dragon blood to be dormant for generations. It makes it unlikely you are the only one who has the ability to use dragon magic."

"And yet you are certain you can't?" I asked.

Shayla nodded. "Positive."

"Well, thank you for the clarification. I better get back to Alpenglow palace."

Shayla stood. "I'll walk you out."

CHAPTER 23 - DETERMINATION

"This cursed thing doesn't work right," I complained as I tapped the hearing aid. The tapping did little more than provide another irritating sound that cemented my dislike and disappointment in the hearing aids. They weren't like the prosthetic eye, which provided sight with benefits, they provided a poor replacement for sound, which made me miss the authentic thing more.

It had been a few weeks, and there was still no sign of Kayda or the clone that controlled her and tried to kidnap Niko and Rikki. In the quiet, I took the opportunity to get the last surgery to fix my hearing. Now that I was fully recovered, I was enjoying the warm weather next to a pool at Alpenglow palace, where Phoenix was kind enough to allow me and my family to stay as we searched for Kayda.

Phoenix laughed, a metallic grating sound that little resembled what I recalled her laugh sounding like. I truly hated the way every sound had a metallic, static sound. It made wind sound like static, and footsteps sound like louder static.

"It won't perfectly recreate sound as you recall hearing it. Your hearing was completely destroyed," she said.

I took the hearing aids out and tossed them on the small table, then turned to Phoenix. The sounds hurt and didn't sound right. It was exhausting and distracting to figure out what each sound was supposed to be, and I didn't think it was worth the effort when every sound was so grating and horrible.

"I'll keep learning sign language," I announced. While the text feature of my prosthetic eye was helpful, the handful of phrases Nicky and Rikki taught both me and Rowan were more so. It took a little less focus, and while the language was different, it was far more expressive than text, or the static. That the hearing aids send the chip in my brain.

"Keep the hearing aids," Phoenix advised with a long-suffering smile. She held both of my infant toddlers, one on each knee. Calliope stared at me with her wide blue eyes, while Thalia snatched a hearing aid off the table and tried to put it in her mouth.

I leaned forward quickly, and I used my finger to flick the hearing aid out of her mouth, then moved both hearing aids out of the reach of either of my girls. I glared at Calliope. While they were still babies, I long suspected that Calliope's quiet, gentler nature was a cover so she could distract me, her father, or any that watched the twins, and enable her sister to cause the chaos she thrived in.

Thalia squawked, and Phoenix responded by bouncing both girls a little more, calming them with an expert hand that made me wonder if children were in her near future. Considering how close she was with her soulmate, Tai, it was likely.

"I don't know who's going to be more trouble, these two adorable little girls, or those two," Phoenix nodded to what she saw behind me. I turned, in time to see Athena in the process of teaching Dani the best places to stab an opponent for maximum pain. She was a patient instructor, and Dani was an enthusiastic student.

"Eh, you should have done a better job of convincing my parents that I really am a bad influence," I said off handedly. "You should have known I would raise a troublemaker, who would then inspire any kindred spirit, like my sister."

Phoenix sat back and cuddled with the two babies. She stared at the palace, lost in thought. I didn't need to ask her to know she was thinking of Kayda, and the chaos that was coming.

"We might need troublemakers," Phoenix admitted, facing me.

BOOKS BY THIS AUTHOR

Dragon's Soulmate

Read the events of Dragon's Sacrifice from Phoenix's point of view

Dragon's Gambit

Dragon's Loyalty

A kindle vella coming soon to ebook format

Sapphire Marionette

Topaz Royalty

Mars' Diamond

Autumn Phoenix

www.ingramcontent.com/pod-product-compliance
Lightning Source LLC
Chambersburg PA
CBHW072102150726
47999CB00005B/1850